Paradise House

Paradise House
K. M. Peyton

SCHOLASTIC

First published in the UK in 2011 by Scholastic Children's Books
An imprint of Scholastic Ltd
Euston House, 24 Eversholt Street
London, NW1 1DB, UK
Registered office: Westfield Road, Southam, Warwickshire, CV47 0RA
SCHOLASTIC and associated logos are trademarks
and/or registered trademarks of Scholastic Inc.

Text © K. M. Peyton, 2011

The right of K. M. Peyton to be identified as the author
of this work has been asserted by her.

ISBN 9781407116648

A CIP catalogue record for this book
is available from the British Library.

Printed in the UK by CPI Bookmarque, Croydon, Surrey.

Papers used by Scholastic Children's Books are made from
wood grown in sustainable forests.

1 3 5 7 9 10 8 6 4 2

To Micky, with love and gratitude
for our long and happy collaboration
in both books and horses

Chapter One

The woman was so beautiful. She was smiling. She had smiley eyes and smiley white teeth, and gorgeous red-brown hair heaped in curls over her forehead. She wore crimson velvet and sparkling pearls and diamonds, and her arms were stretched out in welcome.

"My Alice! My own little Alice!" she said.

She smelled delicious, of lily of the valley.

Alice ran into her arms, and the woman dissolved.

Alice banged her head on the mahogany bedhead and woke up, reeling with the sense of belonging, of being loved, of being wanted.

How strange!

She wasn't loved or wanted. She didn't know what it felt like. For a magic moment, in the dream, she found out. She tried desperately to hold on, to savour the warmth of the open arms, the smell of the perfume, the loving eyes. But the dream faded as dreams always do. It slipped away; the soft voice faded.

Alice, wide awake, felt as if someone had died.

But no one she knew could elicit the same sense of loss as she had just experienced.

She lay staring at the ceiling.

Monday. Poo! Cold meat and boiled cabbage. The smell of polish. The cold parlour and French with Miss Pratt.

Her father wouldn't let her go to school. No reason why.

"When I say no, I mean it. It's not for you to question my decisions."

His decision. Her life, though.

No school friends then. Her only friends were Mabel the housemaid and Robin, the groom's son out in the back yard. Mrs Pinney, the housekeeper-cum-cook, was old and strict but not bad. Not really a friend, though. She reported on Alice's rudeness and disobedience to Alice's father and he would order her to be shut in her room on bread and water for the day. Mabel might sneak up with a jam tart when no one was looking.

But none of these people would open their arms to her like the lady in the dream and call her *my Alice*. She wasn't anyone's Alice, as far as she could see. She was only Alice Ticino, daughter of Mr Joe Ticino, the dreary old estate agent who had an office in Newmarket High Street. He never hugged her or kissed her. She had no aunties, uncles or cousins – or none that she had heard of. Joe Ticino wasn't into relations. All his acquaintances were "business" – land owners, farm bailiffs, builders and suchlike. His wife, Alice's mother, had died when Alice was two. Alice didn't remember her at all. Mr Ticino never mentioned his wife's name. Mrs Pinney said she had been an orphan and had no relations, so Alice got no presents, no birthday cards, no visits. And if Mr Ticino had any relations, Alice certainly didn't know about them. He was a cold and taciturn man, without emotion.

So Alice was tough. But sometimes she longed for the hugs and kisses of her dream. When she saw mothers in the town hugging their children and laughing with them, she always felt a cold stab in the heart.

Mrs Pinney said she was a "hard little thing".

She didn't see it was a cover-up.

Sometimes Alice cried in bed. No one ever heard her. The house was large and cold. Mrs Pinney and Mabel had rooms in the attic. Mr Ticino was in his study drinking whisky and reading the racing results. Alice was sent to bed strictly at seven o'clock. She was *eleven*. After dinner she read books in the study with her silent father. At seven, as soon as the clock had finished chiming, he would say, "Goodnight, Alice."

"Goodnight, Father."

No kiss, not even a smile. His eyes did not leave the paper.

She would climb up to the freezing bathroom and clean her teeth. She didn't wash; he wouldn't notice. Mrs Pinney said if she didn't clean her teeth she would have to go to the dentist. Alice knew that one suffered agony at the dentist. Mabel had told her. Buckets of blood. Screams. They held you down. She could do without that. No one said your head dropped off if you didn't wash. She left washing until the morning. Once a fortnight Mrs Pinney washed her hair, which was terrible. Such a knocking and rubbing and soap in the eyes. Her hair was so long and thick and curling. "Like washing the hall mat," Mrs Pinney would say, her knuckles cracking amongst the lather. It was the same colour as that of the lady of her dreams, reddish-brown, and the same curls. But Alice had to have hers tightly braided, screwed back from her high, bright forehead by Mrs Pinney's hard hands, so that even her eyes got pulled up wide open, green and surprised, blinking tears.

Alice lay looking at the ceiling, woken from her lovely dream. The day was hardly welcoming. Newmarket was a cold place, with icy winds from the east. The windows in the Ticino house rattled in the wind and the draught made billowing sails of the sad curtains. Brown curtains, brown carpets, beige wallpaper with grey-pink roses – who chose it? Alice wondered. Her mother? It was all old and faded.

I hate this house, Alice thought.

She had glimpses of others in the street when coming home from her walk with Mabel in the dusk, before the curtains were pulled. She saw brighter rooms, dancing fires, crimson wallpaper, children in pretty bright dresses with coloured hair ribbons. Alice's dresses were all beige and navy blue, so as not to show the dirt.

"You're such a dirty child," Mrs Pinney always said firmly.

She played in the stable-yard with Robin whenever she got the chance, and rode the pony that pulled the lawnmower. She did get a bit dirty. But it was the only nice thing she did in the whole of her life. The rest was all lessons and healthy walks and sewing and learning the beastly piano, and going to church three times on Sunday, with her father in the morning, gloomily to Sunday school in the afternoon, and with Mabel for evensong. Not to burn in hellfire – that was the gist of it. You had to learn what not to do, so as to be happy when you were dead, and go to Paradise. If you weren't good you went to Hell, not a pretty thought. Hell was described in great detail. Flames burnt you, for ever. It was gruesome. It made you be good, to hear all about Hell. It was hard to be good. You had to say, "God forgive us miserable sinners" every Sunday, even when you couldn't think of a single bad thing you had done. And she wasn't that miserable, most of the time. (There was always Robin and the little field where they had their camp, and Mabel filched them a slice of gingerbread and they shared it, to the last crumb.) Alice hated church. Everyone else was in families, and they had lovely mothers in amazing hats. But Alice only had her grim father, who never stopped to talk. He only went because it was good for business, to be seen. That's what Mabel said. He read the racing paper during the sermon, folded up small.

Alice knew she had to get up when the clock struck seven. The clock was loud and rude in the hall, seven feet tall. Alice hated the clock, as well as church, telling her what to do. Every morning her father came down the stairs and checked the gold watch out of his waistcoat pocket against the time on the hall clock. They were always perfectly matched. Why did he bother? Everything he did, he did to time. Exactly. Breakfast at seven-twenty, leave the house at seven-fifty, office at eight. Alice hated time. It was always too long.

She climbed out of bed and struggled into her boring clothes: her long drawers and flannel petticoats and Spencer and bust-bodice and the boring brown top with buttons all the way up and hooks and eyes round the side and the black boots with more hooks and buttons. Layers and layers. The house was freezing, but at least she wasn't going to freeze to death. Mrs Pinney would do her hair in the kitchen, along with the porridge. At least it was warm in the kitchen. The range stayed on all night, to cook the porridge and heat the water. Mrs Pinney took a jug of hot water up to Mr Ticino every morning, for his shave, but she couldn't be bothered for Alice. So Alice gave herself a sketchy wipe-over in the kitchen. She had a bath once a week. That was enough, surely?

Mrs Pinney had good news.

"Miss Pratt isn't coming this morning. She's not well."

"Oh good!"

"That's very unkind!"

"I meant good she's not coming. Not good she's unwell."

"Well, you just keep out of my way. I've got to take up the parlour carpet today and clean underneath, and I don't want you pestering me."

"No, I won't. I'll go out."

The sun was shining but it was still cold. It was spring, and the trees behind the house were a brilliant green, just unfolding. Cherry blossom flew about like confetti. As soon as the porridge was eaten and Mr Ticino had departed, Alice put on her playing jacket and ran out into the stable-yard.

"Robin! Robin!"

He was mucking out, forking wet straw into a barrow. Robin was ten, a skinny slip of an underfed, overworked live wire with a grin like the Cheshire Cat and a face freckled like a blackbird's egg. His elder brothers were racehorse "lads" and he was going to be one himself as soon as he was twelve. Or sooner. As soon as he was out of school. As far as Alice could see he was rarely in it. His father, Mr Ticino's groom, was never in when the school inspector called, and his mother, like Alice's, was in the graveyard.

"I've got the day off! Miss Pratt is ill!"

"Oh good. You can come to the forge with me. I've got to take Daisy."

Daisy was Mr Ticino's gig horse, a gaunt, long-legged bay mare that he drove when he had business out of town. Alice and Robin had christened her Daisy after one of the Prince of Wales's lady friends; otherwise she was just called "the mare". Alice was allowed to ride her when her father didn't want her, one of the few treats in her life. Robin rode about on Patter, the lawnmower pony, when he wasn't working. Robin only weighed twenty-five kilograms and didn't eat much because he wanted to be a jockey. Alice was half as heavy again at the same age, although she said a lot of it was clothes.

"Well, I don't want to be a jockey."

(The woman in the dream had been curvaceous in a most beautiful way, her rounded, pink arms creaming out of the

7

dark velvet. She came back to Alice with a stab, as she stood before Robin.)

"If Mr Ticino doesn't use Daisy tomorrow, and Miss Pratt is still ill, we could ride to the races," Robin said.

Alice caught her breath.

"Don't tell my father! He would never allow it!"

"No, why should he know?" Robin was scornful. "If you're frightened—"

"I'm not frightened!"

"Well then. . ."

This was often the way with Robin. He dared her, and was scornful if she was afraid.

She loved race days, when all the nobility came to town. Ladies like the lady in her dream . . . they came in their private carriages, or on the train from London, in all their finery, with the dukes and their lordships and their retinues of servants. What a spectacle! Even Mrs Pinney and Mabel went out to have a look. They went up to the station to see the toffs getting off the train. They took Alice sometimes and pointed out famous people. Once they saw the Prince of Wales himself!

Father went to the races but he wouldn't take Alice. It was all right for ladies to go to the races, but not alone. Well, she would go with Robin. Her father stayed in the betting ring. He was unlikely to see her. Mrs Pinney would let her go, but would say she must make sure her father didn't see her.

"Perhaps Miss Pratt will die," Robin said hopefully.

"That's wicked!"

Robin laughed.

"Surely you know everything there is to know by now, with lessons on your own?"

"How can you ever know everything?"

"What matters, I mean."

Robin said at school they sat in rows, ninety of them in one class, with their hands on their desks, and if they got an answer wrong the master hit them with his cane. *Wham!*

At least Miss Pratt only scolded. She didn't wham. She had a voice like a bluebottle.

But Robin could read and write and say all his tables. It was self-preservation, so as not to be whammed. Alice used to hear them when she passed by the school on a summer's day. Through the open windows, the chanting of, "eight nines are seventy-two, nine nines are eighty-one, ten nines are ninety. . ." All the boys in one building, all the girls in another, chanting away. Alice longed, longed, to be there with the girls, chanting. Even with the threat of being whammed. On the blackboard she could see the spelling words written up: "Symmetry, parallel, siege, receive, guard. . ." Oh, she knew them all! She would never get whammed. She would get rewarded with a prize at the end of term, a holy picture of Jesus in Paradise, surrounded by gold stars. How glorious it would be!

Robin emptied the wheelbarrow on the manure heap and fetched Daisy's bridle from the tack room. The stable-yard was at the bottom of the garden. It was small and poky, its gate giving on to a back lane. Beside it was a little field, skirted with high flowering hawthorn, full of daisies, where they played. Beyond the field were more back gardens and other people's stables, mostly more grand than theirs. Most of the people in the road were grander than they were.

Alice had once heard someone wondering how her father could afford a house "grander than his station". This was outside church one day. The other person had said, "Don't you know the reason? It's because——" But Mabel had jerked her away with such a start that she never heard the rest.

She went to the forge with Robin and Daisy. It was only down the lane and round the corner.

The blacksmith laughed at them and said, "Brought 'er to 'ave 'er racing plates on then?"

"I'm going to ride her to the races tomorrow," Alice boasted proudly.

"Aye, well, watch you don't win by too far, Miss Alice, else your 'andicap'll go up."

Alice didn't see the joke, but smiled politely.

That night she prayed for Miss Pratt – to go on being ill.

Chapter Two

"Miss Pratt has pleurisy," Mrs Pinney announced the next morning.

The power of prayer was amazing!

Alice tried to look downcast, not very successfully. "Poor Miss Pratt!"

She could not hide the gleam in her eyes.

"Then I can go out today?"

"Unless you want to clean the silver?"

Mrs Pinney was a bad tease, and Alice had not yet learned to see through her. Her heart plummeted into her boots, until Mabel, taking pity, said, "There, she doesn't mean it!" Alice looked up and saw Mrs Pinney laughing at her. Alice never could work out Mrs Pinney. She was kind, but took great care not to show it. She was the nearest Alice could get to a mother, and a great disappointment in that direction. But you could depend on her. She was a rock in more senses than one.

"If I'm not mistaken, you want to ride Daisy out to the racecourse? With that little brat Robin?"

Alice said nothing, biting her lip.

"Daisy's safe as houses," Mabel said encouragingly. "Alice will see everything from up there."

"Yes, as long as she keeps out of the way. Remember, madam, keep well away from the carriages and the roisterers. You know what I mean!"

"Yes, Pinney." (She was allowed to dispense with the Mrs. Mrs Pinney wasn't married, anyway.)

"And leave at half-past three, before all the traffic. I shall expect you back here at four. Else there'll be no tea and no supper either."

"Yes, Pinney."

Oh, what a day! She had dreaded Mrs Pinney saying no. To show willing she did offer to clean some silver first, but Mrs Pinney said it would be better if she did some lessons in the study. Miss Pratt, for all her pains, had sent work by a messenger boy, so Alice diligently learned the dates of the Plantagenet kings and who was who in the Wars of the Roses, and the exports of Chile and Peru in the nineteenth century and why there was no tide in the Mediterranean sea, before she went to change into her riding habit. She bulged a bit in her habit these days and Mrs Pinney said she'd be much improved when she went into corsets. Alice breathed in hard, pretending corsets, and did up the straining buttons.

"There!"

"Quite a lady," sniffed Mrs Pinney.

She and Mabel were going down the high street to see the toffs arrive: it was their treat too.

"But you go the back way. No high street! We don't want you getting in the way of their Lordships!"

"Yes, Pinney!"

She flew out of the back door like a bird from its cage. It was a fine spring day with puffy white clouds scudding across an azure sky. The amiable Daisy already had her side saddle on, ready and waiting in the stable, and Patter, the little black lawnmower pony, was brushed off and ready to go, tied up beside her. Robin's father, Tom, was gardening next door. He came and bunked her into the saddle. He was a very easy-going man, always cheerful. He looked after Daisy and Patter and did gardening along the road. He had once been a racehorse "lad" but now his rheumatism was too bad for that.

"Mind you don't win now," he said to Alice. Just like the blacksmith.

Daisy was really a carriage horse, a good trotter with a high-stepping action, a shining bay with a white blaze. She was very well-mannered, and now quite old, very easy to ride. She never did anything wrong, which was why Alice was allowed to ride her out. "Safer on that horse than on her feet," Pinney said to Mabel, in Alice's hearing.

So they rode out of town by the back way and crossed the Cambridge road on to the heath where the races were run. The Cambridge road was chock-a-block with traffic but, once across, the familiar horizons of green turf to the skyline opened up before them, as far as the eye could see. . . Even Daisy tossed her head with delight. In the distance the

13

grandstand stood proud and they could see the ant-like turmoil around it, the carriages parking along the course-side, the betting rings opening up and the first runners coming up from the town, pirouetting across the grass in their coloured rugs and hoods. This was where they must not go.

"We'll go to the start and get a good view of all the jockeys pushing and swearing," Robin said. "I like that best! Let's canter!"

So they turned to canter well clear of the far side of the course towards the distant start line. The Newmarket course was straight, not a circle like most, and nobody in the grandstand could see the start, only the finish. Spectators on horseback usually rode up to the start and followed the race down, many racing each other. Another thing they MUST NOT do, Alice knew. These people included the "roisterers", as Pinney called them.

Patter had to gallop on his short little legs to keep up with Daisy's lolloping canter. Robin broke into song,

> "Camptown races, sing this song,
> Doo-dah! Doo-dah!
> Camptown races, five miles long,
> Doo-dah doo-dah daaay!"

Patter was galloping as fast as he could go. Robin put his face into the wind and bawled,

> "GWINE to run all night!
> GWINE to run all day!
> Camptown races five miles long,
> somebody bet on de bay!"

Alice joined in,

> "GWINE to run all night!
> GWINE to run all day!"

She had a stitch, she was laughing so much. A button on her tight jacket popped and flew away. Laughing and singing, "What's GWINE?" she asked.

"We're GWINE to the races," Robin cried.

They couldn't stop laughing. Thank goodness there was no one to see them. Oh, the bliss of it! Instead of Miss Pratt and the Plantagenet kings.

When the jockeys came down for the first race there were quite a few riders at the start: farmers on their cobs, smartish gentlemen on their hunters and the usual "roisterers" – mostly undergraduates from Cambridge – on hirelings. The start was by the fall of a flag. The starter rode down on his horse and a lad held it while he climbed up on his little rostrum. The racehorses were young and skittish and lining them up fairly was a terrible job. There were three false starts. The roisterers jeered and shouted. The starter roared at them. The jockeys shouted, "No, sir! No, sir!"

Robin watched, entranced. It was his whole life's ambition to be a jockey. He spent a lot of time in the stables where one of his brothers worked, a famous stable on the edge of town.

From Daisy's back, Alice had a fine view of the goings-on. When the race was finally started, they cantered down behind all the others, very sedate, and pulled up when they got to the first of the spectators on the rails. They could see the racehorses coming back after the race was run, silhouetted on the far side of the stands, still prancing. Their lads ran out to meet them.

Robin wanted to be the lad of a winner, and lead it in amongst the cheering crowds. It was his other ambition, if he wasn't good enough to make a jockey. His eyes gleamed at the sight. Back in town, his class at school was learning how cotton was grown and why it came to be processed in Lancashire where the air was damp and the cotton didn't snap in the spinning of it. "I don't want to know all that stuff," Robin said. "Not to work in a stable."

His father said he was pig-ignorant, and laughed.

After the big race, Alice knew she would have to start for home. They rode up to the start for the third time and watched the famous horses lobbing up towards them, the stars of racing. They belonged to the dukes and their Lordships, the Prince of Wales, the famous Joels and Rothschilds, the richest men in the world. They lined up, their jockeys jostling and swearing. Alice sat behind the throng, watching, while Daisy grazed.

16

They all went off and the followers started to move. Alice was just about to gather up her reins when, suddenly, Daisy threw up her head, gave a great convulsive leap into the air and set off down the course at full gallop. Her ears were flat down on her head and she felt to Alice as if she had gone mad.

Alice was so surprised it took her some time to gather her trailing reins and try to get Daisy to stop. She went past several gentlemen and even some of the roisterers, who shouted after her, "Make way! Make way! Here comes the winner!"

"Oh, please God, make her stop!" Alice prayed, when her own efforts had no effect at all. Daisy's head was stretched out before her and her hooves pounded the hard turf. She was right in the middle of the racecourse and soon the first spectators were cheering her on. Alice was now white with terror, not so much with physical fear but with the horrors of charging into all their Lordships and nobility who milled about the course ahead of her. The name of the winner was being shouted, and lads running out on to the course had to spring back as Daisy came through. Some men waved their arms in front of her and Daisy veered into the spectators. Alice shut her eyes and screamed.

With people all around her, Daisy pulled up in a series of back-breaking leaps, while several men now hung on to her reins. Some were tossed aside and went flying. They were into the crowd waiting to receive the winners and Alice saw duchesses jumping back in alarm, ladyships screaming and famous trainers bounding nimbly aside.

With so many people underfoot, Daisy at last pulled up. Alice, sobbing, was lifted from the saddle and a crowd gathered round her as great as round the winner of the race. A huge hubbub ensued, arms waving and roisterers shoving in to get a look. From low down Robin appeared, leading Patter.

"A bee stung her. She ate it," he said, but no one heard him.

An authoritative man said to Robin, "Who is she? Your sister?"

"She's Alice Ticino. It's not her fault. A bee stung her horse."

"Alice Ticino!"

The man was a trainer whom one of Robin's brothers worked for. He recognized Robin and said to him, "Take the horse. I'll see to the girl."

He took Alice by the arm and said to everyone, "Leave her alone. I'll see to her. I know who she is."

And, putting a strong arm round Alice's shoulders, he directed her out of the press. A woman whom Alice presumed was his wife, trailing several children, came to meet him and said, "What an upset! Lucky no one was hurt! Is the child alone?"

"It's Alice Ticino," the trainer said.

"Alice!"

The woman stopped in her tracks. Alice looked up and saw an extraordinary expression pass over the woman's face, of shock and concern. Compassion, she would have said (a word she knew how to spell). Why didn't she just say in a Mrs Pinney sort of voice, "Alice Ticino, eh?", implying, "I'll give her what for. Making an exhibition of herself!" This was what

18

Alice had expected. She was limp with shame at what she had done. But the woman put her arm round her and said, "My poor love, what a shock for you."

Comforted, Alice looked up and found herself surrounded by the four children of Mrs Scott, the trainer's wife. Three girls and a boy. Alice knew them by sight, from church, and riding around, and knew quite a lot about them from Robin. The boy was called William. He was the second eldest, and was the same age as Alice. He was very clever and liked books better than horses. This had been reported with great astonishment. He had a private tutor, a different one from the girls, Robin said. The girls were all blonde and blue-eyed but William had dark reddish-brown hair rather like Alice's own, and thoughtful hazel eyes.

Alice said, "Daisy's a good horse. She's never done that before – never!"

Mrs Scott said – and she should know – "Unpredictable creatures, horses, my dear. What a blessing no harm came to you. Well, well, you'd better stay with me for the time being, and I'll see you home after the next race. We've a runner in that."

Although glad to be comforted, Alice was not glad at all at the prospect of having to stay with the Scott children instead of larking about with Robin. The only good thing was that Mrs Scott might stop the wrath of God descending on her when her father heard about the escapade, as he was bound to. He might even have witnessed it and kept his head down. But the superior children of one of the best trainers in town made difficult company.

Ellen, the eldest, about fourteen, looked at her as if she were a piece of bad cheese and said, "Was that a carriage horse you were riding?"

"My father's horse. She's lovely."

"Funny-looking thing for hacking!"

Of course the Scott girls all rode around Newmarket in beautiful habits on thoroughbred ponies.

William said, "The boy said a bee stung her. That must have been really scary, coming down the course like that!"

"Were you frightened?" asked the youngest child.

"Only of trampling a duchess or somebody."

William laughed. "Do some of them good," he said.

"Really, Will!" sniffed Ellen. "It could have been dreadful!"

How quickly one found out one's friends! The second girl, Amelia, said nothing but gave Alice a confidential smile as if she were agreeing with William. In no time at all Alice decided that she and the boy were all right, Ellen was ghastly, and the others too little to bother about. But Ellen impressed her authority on all of them. William – presumably because he was a boy – ignored her, but the others all jumped to her commands.

Ellen said, "What does your father do?"

Do? Alice wondered. Whatever did she mean?

"He gets up, has his breakfast, reads the racing paper, goes to work. . ."

William and Amelia grinned.

"What work does he do, I mean, stupid?"

Alice had no idea. "He goes to an office. He drives out quite a lot, to look at buildings. I don't know what for."

"He's an estate agent, Ellen," William said. "You are thick. Father's worked with him. You know perfectly well."

They were all trailing after Mrs Scott towards where the runners for the next race were being led round. Robin had made himself scarce with Daisy. Alice wondered about skiving off to look for him, but decided that being taken home by Mrs Scott might be a better bet. She was in for big trouble either way. She might as well make the best of it. At least she was in with the nobility and getting a really close-up view of the people Pinney and Mabel gaped at in the high street. The owner of the runner Mr Scott was now saddling was called "Your Grace". That meant a duke. Alice knew that at least. His lady (wife? One never knew, according to Pinney) was deliciously dressed in turquoise silk with the smallest (most corseted) waist Alice had ever seen. It was stunning! Diamond pendants swung from her ears, and a hat like the nest of a bird of paradise perched above swathes of upswept curls. Close up, she smelled of roses. Alice could see she wore powder and rouge – how shocking! Alice stared. To tell Pinney and Mabel – they would love it!

Ellen kicked her quite hard on the ankle and said, "Don't stare!"

Alice jumped. She went red and stared at the horse instead. It looked so delicate! So beautiful! Even a duchess couldn't hold a candle to a good thoroughbred, Robin's father said. It was true. And the jockey – the most famous in the land – so close she could have touched him! Hollow white cheeks and those sad grey eyes that made all the ladies fall in love with him. His wife had died in childbirth and left him heartbroken. Alice knew all the gossip and now here she was right in the middle of it! What a day! Surely she could stare at the jockey?

Mr Scott legged him into the saddle.

Their own duke and duchess turned to chat with some more diamond-dripping owners and the horse disappeared through the throng on to the course.

"Come along," said Mrs Scott to her brood. "We'll watch from the grandstand, and then we'll go home."

Alice was included. She sat in the grandstand with all the nobility and trainers and saw the famous jockey win. She went down to congratulate him. She was included in all the smiles and rejoicing. The duchess threw her an excited smile. Perhaps the duke would buy the lady another diamond necklace with his winnings? Or two? How lovely it all was! Like a dream. Like the dream of her lady calling her *my Alice*. The lady in her dream was just such a one, but even more beautiful than these real ones. Alice hung on grimly to the details of her wonderful day, to tell Pinney and Mabel.

They left the course in the family barouche behind a pair of beautifully matched chestnuts.

"I will see you in, my dear, and explain what happened. The least I can do," said Mrs Scott.

The barouche pulled up outside the front door of Alice's house and Mrs Scott told the groom to wait for her. To the children she said, "Get out and run along home. I won't be long."

They all scrambled out. As they departed William turned and grinned and said, "Good luck!"

Very perceptive of him, Alice thought, to know she was going to need it. Ellen didn't even say goodbye. Amelia did.

Mrs Pinney was amazed at Alice appearing at the front door with Mrs Scott. She asked her into the parlour. Mr Ticino wasn't back yet.

"Although he always returns straight after the last race, ma'am. He shouldn't be long. Shall I make you some tea?"

"That would be nice. I really need to speak with him. I'll wait."

Alice was chivvied out and went back to the kitchen with Mrs Pinney.

"Whatever's going on?" Mrs Pinney hissed. "What have you been up to, for goodness' sake?"

Alice explained.

Mrs Pinney rolled her eyes to heaven. "Mrs Scott, of all people! Oh my sainted aunt! What a pickle! Your father will go mad!"

"Why? She was very kind!"

But Pinney went on tut-tutting and saying, "Of all people! Oh my Gawd!"

Alice thought she'd gone mad.

Mrs Pinney took the tea tray to the parlour. When she came back she was so on edge that Alice decided to postpone telling her about the nobility until she was in a fit state to listen. She was on the alert for Mr Ticino's key in the front door. It was not long in coming. Mrs Pinney ran out into the hall.

"Oh, sir, something's happened! Mrs Scott is in the parlour. She wants to speak to you!"

Alice quite clearly heard her father say, in tones of alarm just like Pinney, "Mrs Scott! My God, what does she want?"

But Alice never found out what Mrs Scott wanted. She talked with her father for nearly an hour. When she departed she looked sad, disappointed, Alice would have said, and her father looked as if he had had a very hard day. He sent for a glass of the medicinal brandy out of the kitchen cabinet. When she went to bed that night – amazingly, after no punishment for her day at the races – Mr Ticino said to her, "You are happy here, aren't you, Alice?"

Alice, too astonished to think otherwise, said, "Yes."

Her father said, "Good girl."

Alice nearly fainted.

Then he said, as usual, "Goodnight."

That night Alice dreamed of the lady again, the creamy arms stretching towards her and the soft, smiling mouth saying, "My Alice, my little Alice!"

There was happiness in her dream, she recognized, that she knew nothing about.

Whatever had her father meant?

Chapter Three

Alice woke early the next morning and lay thinking.

Was she happy?

How could one tell? She didn't go around crying, like poor Mabel when she first came to work. Mabel had come at fourteen, up from the country "into service", and had cried every night for weeks, so homesick for her farm home and twelve brothers and sisters. Oh, how she had cried! Her bed in the attic was exactly above Alice's. Great wracking sobs, night after night. The ceiling shook. That was unhappy, Alice supposed. Although now, four years on, she was usually cheerful and laughing, in spite of being bullied by Pinney, and had a "lad" for a boyfriend, who lurked outside the back gates on his afternoons off, whistling a special song. Now she came to think of it, the song was "Camptown Races". That's where Robin had got it from!

What a lark! "GWINE to run all night, GWINE to run all day!" Robin was a laugh. What fun it had been until the bee struck!

And even then, it had been interesting. Those Scotts, save for stuck-up Ellen . . . William and Amelia, well, she could be friends with them. She only had Robin for a friend, and she knew perfectly well he was "unsuitable". Not so unsuitable that he wasn't allowed, but just (sniff, sniff from Pinney) unsuitable. A servant. Alice loved Robin. The only one she could think of to love. She supposed she loved her father, but only because one was supposed to. Really she preferred Mabel and even Mrs Pinney to him, and Robin's dad, Tom. What wicked thoughts! Alice prayed for a bit, asking forgiveness for wicked thoughts. But it was God's fault she didn't have a mother. Her mother rested in God's bosom. Lucky old her! In church they made it sort of lucky, dying, going to eternal rest and peace. But a bit boring if you were young, she thought. There were things to do first. As long as you kept on the right side of God. That was very important.

But why had Mrs Scott's visit made her father call for the medicinal brandy?

Yesterday had been full of very odd behaviour, not just her own. That look of Mrs Scott's — "Alice Ticino!" Mrs Pinney going potty and saying, "Oh my Gawd!" — strictly NOT allowed.

Alice supposed it was true, as they were forever telling her smugly, that she would "understand these things when you're older". What was the dog doing in the yard with next door's terrier, Bella? How could Amy, the maid next door, have a baby when she had no husband? When she asked these questions they always said the same thing. But Miss Pratt said she should have an enquiring mind. Yet, when she enquired, Miss Pratt went right as a beetroot. All very strange.

Alice could hear Mabel and Mrs Pinney getting up in the attic. Although their house was fairly new, you could hear quite well through the walls. It was plain, four-square, fronting on to a quiet street behind the high street, with a privet hedge in front and laurels under the windows. Although Mr Ticino liked to drive away from the front door, to show the neighbours, he never did because to get to the front door from the stable-yard one had to go out of the back lane, all the way down to the bottom, round the corner and all the way back again to the front door. So he drove out of the back lane and disappeared without anyone seeing. The back lane was quiet and overhung with big elms, and led out to the racehorse gallops and the big racing stables on the edge of town. She felt happier when she was out the back, with Robin, messing about. But most of the time . . . was she happy? She supposed she wasn't, very.

What would her father have said if she'd said no?

Were the Scott children happy? Yes, they must be, in their pretty clothes, going out amongst the nobility, riding their beautiful ponies, having a rich father.

Mr Ticino wasn't rich.

Alice knew that because she heard him telling Mrs Pinney she couldn't have this and that, it was too expensive. No new carpet in the dining room, no newfangled electricity. Daisy wanted a new collar. The gig was crocky too and Tom said one day the wheels would fall off and then Mr Ticino would be sorry. Robin and Alice thought this was very funny, Daisy

27

pulling the gig with the wheels fallen off. Worse, no pretty clothes for Alice. Just hard-wearing dark serge with room to grow into. Ellen had been wearing a really pretty white dress with pink roses at the waist and a straw hat with another pink rose in it. William had worn a proper suit with a stiff collar, of much nicer material than that of Mr Ticino's best.

Oh, to have a white dress with pink roses! Or red velvet and pearls! A carpet in her bedroom, instead of cold brown linoleum!

I'm unhappy! thought Alice.

But over breakfast she didn't dare say she had changed her mind. Her father was quiet as usual. Everything was very boring again. But luckily Miss Pratt was still ill. It was raining. Mrs Pinney said she could make rock cakes in the kitchen with Mabel.

"They'll be rock cakes all right if she makes them," Mabel said.

"I'll make fairy cakes then."

"Whichever you like. But edible, please," said Pinney. "My teeth aren't what they used to be."

That was true enough. There weren't many left. Mrs Pinney was old. Alice couldn't tell how old, but her hair was grey and stringy. She was stringy all over. She had a really old mother who lived in a one-up, one-down in the next street, and Pinney had to run out quite often to see she hadn't fallen downstairs or out of bed or whatever, and take her bits of meals in a covered dish. Sometimes Pinney stayed the night there, sleeping on the floor. Sometimes when she was busy she sent Alice with some food, but Alice hated going. The old lady was smelly and horrid. She squawked at Alice and Alice couldn't understand a word she said. She would dump the food and run. Pinney always said to hurry, because she knew Mr Ticino would be angry if he knew she sent Alice. "Don't tell him," Pinney said to her sometimes. But in a soft, sad voice, not her usual bossy one. Was Pinney happy? Alice wondered. Best not to ask. She would get her head snapped off. Mabel said Pinney's mother would be "best out of it". In God's bosom, Alice supposed. (Poor God!)

They were halfway through the fairy cakes when there was a ring at the front bell and Mabel had to go and answer. Her hands were all floury. She came back in a tizzy, holding a letter addressed to Mr Ticino.

"A footman fellow, very smart," she said. "From Mrs Scott, he said."

They burned to know what it said.

Mrs Pinney held it up to the window but there was no seeing through the rich, thick envelope. The writing was very elegant.

"You set the cat amongst the pigeons yesterday and no mistake," Pinney said to Alice crossly. "Better if you'd smacked into the Prince of Wales than that lot!"

"I didn't choose," said Alice.

She nearly added, "It was God's will," but was afraid Mrs Pinney would clip her one.

The letter was left on the silver plate on the hall table.

When Mr Ticino came in he picked it up in surprise and took it into his study. When supper time came and Mrs Pinney brought the dinner into the dining room where Alice ate glumly with her father, he said to her: "Mrs Pinney, I have received a note from Mrs Scott inviting Alice to her eldest daughter's birthday party next week. Do you think she should go?"

"Oh my word!" said Mrs Pinney. She looked flustered. "I'm sure I don't know, sir."

"Nor do I."

"Why not?" Alice shouted.

They ignored her.

"She can't be under wraps for ever. I'm sure Mrs Scott will be very discreet."

Discreet? Alice wasn't sure what it meant (although she knew how to spell it.)

"She's got her life to live, after all," Mrs Pinney said. "She doesn't get much fun with other children."

Mrs Pinney was on her side! Good old Pinney!

"I'll think about it. If you agree, perhaps."

"She's got nothing to wear, sir."

"Well, perhaps you could remedy that. Nothing too expensive, mind."

"When is it, sir?"

"Next Wednesday."

"Very good, sir."

Mrs Pinney went out and Alice said, "Can I go? Please!"

"I think so."

He didn't smile or enthuse. Alice knew better than to leap up and fling her arms round his neck. But it was hard to sit still, the excitement twitching through her body. A party! She had read about parties, but only been to Sunday school parties where they sang hymns and ate jelly, but didn't play. She knew that at proper parties like the Scotts' you played games and hid in the dark and acted charades.

Her father ate his stew as if nothing had happened, the racing paper propped up on the sauce bottle. Was he happy, Alice wondered? You could never tell because he was always the same – quiet, inscrutable, boring. He was a small man with a pale face, spectacles, and grey hair brushed back. No whiskers. Really boring dark clothes. Very precise in his ways. He always unfolded and folded his napkin in exactly the same way; he never left things lying about, or raised his voice. The most perturbed Alice had ever seen him was last night after Mrs Scott's departure. If he had friends, they never came to the house. He went to the Rutland Arms sometimes in the evening and presumably met friends there. Did he have any? He certainly knew everyone in town, but that wasn't quite the same. He didn't seem to have any enemies, at least. No one spoke ill of him.

But he had said yes!

Alice was really excited but later began to wonder if it would turn out as good as she hoped. Ellen wasn't going to be nice to her for a start, unless she took her a good present. A present! What? Pinney would have to think of something. Ellen had everything she needed and more besides. Whatever to give her?

"A cake, and when she opens it it's full of maggots," said Robin.

"What a good idea!"

But Mrs Pinney bought a little gold-looking horse, very pretty, mounted on a varnished wooden block.

"It's lovely!" Alice breathed.

She never got presents that weren't strictly useful, apart from uplifting books about Jesus and good children.

They wrapped it up in brown paper and put ribbon round it. The party dress was a slight disappointment. Pinney said, as she never – except this once – went to parties it would have to be used for other things as well, like Sunday school, so it was dark. But at least it was a greeny-blue colour and not brown or grey, and was better than anything else she had. And Pinney said she could wear her hair loose, a rare concession. She had bought some green ribbons to tie it back with.

"Not right back!" said Alice.

"No, well, just the front bits, else you won't see where you're going."

"You'll be like the old sheep dog in the end house," said Mabel. "Walks into lamp posts."

Mabel was sighing with envy: going to a party!

"We have parties at home, a right old knees-up – all the

farm boys get drunk. But not – like – posh, you know," she said. "I've never been to a posh party, even as a maid."

And when the Wednesday afternoon came, Alice found she felt very nervous, and not very happy. She wouldn't know anyone. All the others would be friends.

"Just think of the food," said Mabel comfortingly. "You look a treat," she added. "All the boys will fall for you."

Even Alice was surprised at how different she looked. The dark greeny-blue of the dress made her eyes look much greener than usual, and seemed to make her hair more chestnut. It stood out all round her in its released frenzy – "Like a blooming coconut mat," said Mrs Pinney, trying to damp it down with a wet comb.

"Go on! It's lovely," Mabel said. "So thick! That Miss Ellen's is just thin and pale like an old dishcloth. Yours is like . . . like. . ." Words failed her. "It's really lovely, miss."

Mabel was almost more excited than Alice. Her round red face shone with pleasure.

"Can Mabel come with me? To the house, I mean?" Alice asked, wanting courage.

"Whatever for?"

"Oh please, Mrs Pinney!" cried Mabel.

Mrs Pinney looked cross but said, "It can do no harm. But come straight back, girl. There's jobs to be done."

It was a sharp spring afternoon. The Scotts' place was not very far, down the back lane, across the bottom of the gallops and on to Bury Road. The house stood back behind high walls.

The gates were open and a long drive curved away between shrubberies and lawns on either side. Lilacs were in full bloom and bright azaleas turned their faces to the sun. Beyond were lawns like green velvet, and a croquet course and a tennis court and hothouses bordering a large kitchen garden.

"What a place!" Mabel breathed.

A huge stable-yard lay behind more walls to the left.

"Of course, all the dukes and suchlike visit here all the time to see their horses. It has to be grand, doesn't it?" Mabel sighed.

Alice, never having seen beyond the gates before, was also awed at the sight. They had to stand back as a carriage and a trap bowled past them, carrying children.

"I should have come with Daisy!" Alice said, stricken.

"Oh don't be silly, for five minutes' walk!"

But no one else was on foot.

Alice's heart sank lower and lower and she hardly noticed when Mabel retreated. The front door of the grand house was open, under a load of flowering wisteria. Inside the hall, Ellen stood greeting her guests with her mother beside her, and a butler and a maid, and Amelia dancing about amongst the present wrappings. Ellen was in white again, this time set off with yellow flowers and a yellow sash. Her golden (thin) curls hung round her shoulders. Mrs Scott came forward and said warmly, "I'm so glad you have come, Alice. It was a happy meeting after all, your horse colliding with us! How lucky you came to no harm. It must have been so frightening!"

She was all charm. Ellen raised her superior smile.

Alice held out the darling little horse.

"I've brought you a present."

She watched eagerly as Ellen undid the wrappings and dropped them on the floor.

Ellen stared at the little ornament and said, "I don't really like horses, you know. Just because my father's a trainer. . ."

She didn't even say thank you. Alice went bright red. Mrs Scott was talking to someone else and didn't hear her daughter's rudeness, but Amelia snatched the horse off her and said, "Don't be so horrid, Ellen! It's lovely, it's really lovely!"

If it hadn't been for Amelia, Alice would have turned tail and run. Her heart was crashing with embarrassment. Ellen was now talking with great animation to a girl who had just entered. Amelia – thank goodness! – said to Alice, "Come with me. I'll take your coat."

It was as she'd feared; she didn't know anyone. The other children were all talking excitedly to one another in little groups and running about. All their dresses were pale and gauzy and no good for anything but parties, and Alice stood out like a beacon, dark and unloved. Amelia was as nice as possible but she too had her own friends and soon departed. Alice hid herself behind some ferns and told herself sternly not to cry. Remember the tea!

They played games and picked sides and no one picked her until she was left last. Mrs Scott came and put her arm round her. Alice wanted to die. Then someone called Mrs Scott away and one of the girls, seizing her opportunity, said spitefully to her, "Are you Alice Ticino?"

"Yes."

"I've heard of you," the girl said, looking her over as if she were a horse for sale.

"Why?" said Alice.

"They say—"

"Go and fry your face," said a voice behind them and Alice turned to see William standing there, scowling at the girl. The girl looked startled and disappeared quickly. *Well squashed*, thought Alice.

"Why has she heard of me?"

"Don't ask me," said William with a shrug. "Your antics at the races, I suppose."

"I don't know anybody here. I don't know why I came."

"No, nor me. But I live here, don't I? No choice. Not my cup of tea at all."

Alice noticed that the boy was not in party dress, only wearing normal breeches and a none-too-clean everyday shirt. Although she did not know him at all, Alice really liked William. He seemed to think like she did. She felt at home with him. She was relieved to have someone to talk to, but unfortunately at that moment Mrs Scott came back and said to him tartly, "I told you to dress properly if you want to be included in the party. Otherwise stay in your room."

"I came down to see if tea was served, that's all."

"Well, it's not yet. We're going to have a game of hide-and-seek first, then tea. And if you want any you must come down in a clean shirt, for goodness' sake."

She then turned to Alice again and said in her kind, motherly way, "Come along, Alice. We're not picking sides any more. Ellen wants to play hide-and-seek. You'll enjoy that."

It was more a command than a hope.

Everyone collected in the hall and a girl was chosen to be the seeker. Then they dispersed in giggling groups all over the house to hide. No one included Alice in their group, not even Amelia. Alice wondered whether to go looking for William in his room, but didn't think he'd want her, like everyone else, so she glanced round and hid herself very obviously behind a chair with a pile of coats thrown over it. She pulled some of the coats round her and leaned back against the wall. There was a nice warm carpet underneath her. She could see all the present wrappings still lying on the floor near the door, and could smell the wisteria hanging over the porch.

Nobody found her. Nobody even looked. When the game was over and everyone was going to the dining room for tea Alice was still sitting under her pile of coats.

So what did she do now?

If she leapt out and said, "I've won!" she didn't think there would be an overwhelming response. Nobody was even missing her. She could sit there until everyone came for their coats to go home, and then they would all stare at her. They might say, "So you're Alice Ticino!" in sneering voices. Even if she went in for tea no one would talk to her.

So she sat there for a bit. Then she noticed her little horse present to Ellen lying on its side under the umbrella stand. She got up and went and picked it up. She pressed it lovingly to her chest and could not help a few hot tears falling on its golden coat.

"She doesn't want you!" Alice could hardly believe it.

But she knew just how it felt. Cuddling the little horse fiercely, she ran out of the front door. But to her consternation some carriages were pulled up in the drive outside with the drivers chatting to each other, and they all stared curiously at her sudden appearance. She knew they could see she was crying. So she pulled up short and walked sideways round the house as if she were on an errand. It seemed to be the way to the stable-yard. There was a wall in front of her with closed gates, and a view through of the yard and lads going about their business. Ahead of her, outside the big yard, her path led into a small, old-fashioned yard, once the coach yard. The coach houses were now loose boxes for horses.

Alice hesitated. It was a nice place, homely, a bit like their own. She heard footsteps coming from the house behind her — was someone at last coming to look for her? Without thinking, she went straight to the first loose box, slipped back the bolt and went inside to hide. Hide-and-seek — well, she was still playing. She wanted desperately to be alone. She slid down into the thick straw, cuddled the little gold horse in her hands and wept.

Of course the footsteps went past; no one was looking for her and no one cared where she was. No one was going to come and comfort her. How feeble she was! As if it mattered! There was really no point in crying.

So she stopped and lifted her head, hearing a sudden rustle in the straw. She had thought the box was empty but was surprised to find herself suddenly looking into the face of a very large horse.

"Hello," she said, as it sniffed doubtfully at her hair. The funny rubbery horse lips snuffled at her green ribbons.

Her scruffy hair could be mistaken for hay, after all. She put up her hand and stroked the horse's nose. How beautiful it was! Huge, with a coat like black silk. The black was dappled faintly with golden brown over the flanks, so pretty! God was amazing, what He thought of. The horse's eyes were so dark, almost purple, full of unfathomable horse thoughts.

Alice slithered to her feet and the horse backed off and stared at her. Its ears flicked backwards and forwards uncertainly.

"Look." Alice held out her little gold ornament. "Here's a friend for you. A little tiny one. Do you like it?"

The big horse made a low strange noise in his throat and goggled at the little gold image. Alice laughed.

"Great big thing like you, frightened of this tiny little fellow!" She made an imitation neigh. "Listen, he's talking to you."

Alice walked round the box and sat herself in the very comfortable manger that ran along the far wall. The big horse followed her round, not taking his eyes off the gold model.

"What is your name?"

Alice made the sort of voice she thought the little horse would talk in, a sort of neighy voice.

"How do you do. I would like to be friends."

Alice let out a very good whinny and made the little horse jump and hit the horse on the nose.

The big horse leapt back as if he had been stung like Daisy. Alice laughed.

"I want to be your friend!" she whinnied.

Then she said in her horse voice, "I belong to Alice Ticino now. Beastly Ellen threw me on the floor. So now I'm Alice's. I shall go home with Alice."

Then she said, being Alice again, "You really are so beautiful. I wish you could come home and live with Daisy. Did you win the Derby? Are you famous? Do you belong to the Prince of Wales?"

The horse put out his nose and sniffed her hand. He was beginning to look less goggly. Alice very gently held up the gold horse again and the real horse breathed heavily over it so the gold went all cloudy.

"There, you're friends. I'm afraid I can't introduce you as I don't know your name."

Then, in her horse voice, "How do you do. My name is Goldie."

Not very original, but the best she could manage at short notice.

Then she realized that someone was looking in over the half door from the yard. Not only one person, but three or four, one of them in a bowler hat. They had shocked expressions on their faces.

Alice felt herself going bright red. Sitting there talking in a silly voice, she had forgotten the party and the rest of the world, and her tears. The real world was now looking at her, with much the same expressions on their faces as Ellen's when she had received her present. She was trespassing! This beautiful horse was probably worth ten thousand pounds and Mr Scott would send her home in disgrace!

She jumped down from the manger.

The man in the bowler hat said in a strangled sort of voice, "Don't move! Stand still!"

It made Alice freeze.

"I didn't mean any harm," she said.

The bowler hat man turned to a lad and said, "Send for Mr Scott. Quick as you can!"

"I'm not doing any harm!" Alice wailed again. "I'm from the party. They invited me. I'm a guest."

"Hush," said the man. "Keep quiet and stay still!" Very abrupt.

The crowd behind him seemed to be swelling. The faces were all goggling. Was it because they recognized Alice Ticino, the bolter from the races? How could it be? What had she done? She sensed she was in deep trouble.

41

The crowd suddenly parted and she saw the top half of Mr Scott appear, accompanied by William.

"Hey, gosh, Alice, what are you doing in there?" William said.

"I'm not doing any harm!"

"That's Snatchcorn. He's a killer."

"Be quiet, William!" hissed his father. And to Alice, in ominously silky tones, "Just be a good girl and stay exactly where you are. Don't move."

The horse had turned to face the crowd outside and his large hindquarters were pinning Alice against the manger. He now looked rather different, with his enquiring ears laid flat back on his head and the strange growly noise coming from his throat again. Alice laid her head against the shining flank and started to cry again. What a party! Everything in the world was going wrong.

Then the horse, feeling her hot tears on his tender hide, turned round and reached out his head towards her. She felt his soft nudge against her arm. She heard Mr Scott shout, "Don't move!" What a twit the man was, thought Alice. Such a fuss. She could tell the horse was being nice to her, just like Daisy. When he turned his head to her, his ears went forward and he gave a little whicker in his throat just like Daisy when she saw a carrot. What a pity she didn't have a carrot in the pocket of her green dress.

There was now dead silence from the crowd outside. Even Mr Scott was silent. Released by Snatchcorn's backside, Alice took a hesitant step forward. Was it allowed? She looked at Mr Scott. Silent. Just looking. What an expression on his face! Goggling, like the horse looking at Goldie.

Alice put her hand up and stroked Snatchcorn's face. The horse now had his ears forward and looked thoroughly pleasant. If he were a cat, he would have purred. Alice went round to his front and stroked his neck. It seemed to be the right thing to do. Snatchcorn nuzzled her hand, the one holding Goldie. Alice nearly spoke to him in her Goldie voice, but didn't think it would please Mr Scott. She just said, very softly so that no one could hear, "I love you. You're beautiful."

Mr Scott opened the half door and said in a strangled sort of voice, "Come out, Alice. Come out at once."

Alice came. She knew her time was up. Mr Scott closed the door behind her, and immediately a great hubbub broke out all round her, the lads all exclaiming and pushing in to get a look at her. She was the centre of attention once more! Even some of the party girls were standing in the gateway in their white dresses like a flock of geese. She could see their lips saying, "It's Alice Ticino!"

Mr Scott was scattering his lads with angry words. They all went jostling back to the big yard, chattering excitedly. Alice remained with Mr Scott and the man in the bowler hat and William.

The man in the bowler hat said, "All's well that ends well! Who'd have believed it?"

43

Sweat stood in beads on Mr Scott's forehead. William was looking mightily impressed.

He said, "No one goes in that horse's box without a pitchfork at the ready. Only one man can handle him at all. He killed a lad once, and savaged another man so badly last week that he's still in hospital."

"Well, he likes me," Alice said stoutly. But at William's words her knees went a bit trembly.

"He's going to be put down next month because he's too dangerous."

At this Alice's ill-contained tears burst forth again.

"You can't! You can't kill him! He's so beautiful. And he loves me!"

Mr Scott, together again, put his hand kindly on Alice's shoulder and said, "Well, young lady, it certainly seems that way. Don't cry. Think how lucky you've been that he took so sweetly to you. I've never seen him behave like that in all my life. By jove, what a shock you gave us!"

He steered Alice back towards the house. She turned and gave a last look towards Snatchcorn and through her tears saw him watching her go, his ears pricked up, his nose wrinkling with the faintest whicker.

"Amazing!" said Mr Scott.

Alice cried harder than ever. The day was total disaster. Worse and worse, the flock of geese was in the hall with their eyes out on stalks to see her return.

"I want to go home!" Alice sobbed.

Mrs Scott came running out and Alice buried her head in her voluminous silk skirts, wishing she was back under the pile of coats.

She could hear them all chattering.

"Alice Ticino!"

"Did you see what she did?"

"She's mad!"

"Do you know about her? My mother says—"

"Yes, our maid told me."

"Mr Ticino's not really her father."

Mrs Scott bawled out in a fierce voice, "Go back to the dining room, all of you! At once! Have you no manners at all?"

They all turned and fled.

Alice stayed with her head buried, burning with shock. Through the tears she sobbed, "I want to go home! I want to go home!"

Total, utter disaster.

Chapter Four

They could see she had been crying, but Alice did not say a word about what had happened when she got home. She told them Ellen had thrown the little horse away so she had brought it back with her and its name was Goldie.

"It's mine. I love him."

"What a nerve!" said Mabel. "How rude!"

"Spoilt little madam!" Pinney sniffed.

"What did you play?" Mabel asked.

"Hide-and-seek. I won. Nobody found me."

"Great! And what was for tea? Was it scrumptious?"

"Oh yes, everything you can think of. Jelly, blancmange, trifle, cake. . ." Alice's repertoire of exotic food did not stretch far. "Everything you can think of," she repeated.

She dared not say she was starving hungry.

"You won't want much supper then. I'll just give you a titbit to eat with your father," Pinney said.

Alice's head ached. Everything that had happened spun round in it, round and round until she felt sick. Those girls all in white, goggling. And the excited, perfectly audible whisper, "Mr Ticino's not really her father."

They had sent William to walk her home. He was very impressed with her escapade in the stable. He didn't want to talk about the other things, and Alice did not dare ask him about Mr Ticino not being her father. How would he know?

She dared not ask her father either.

At supper, her meagre portion quickly scoffed, she answered his brief question, "How was the party?"

"Very nice, thank you."

"Good," he said. That was all.

When Pinney was plaiting her hair for bed Alice said, "Someone said Mr Ticino isn't my father."

Yank!

"Ouch!"

"What a ridiculous thing to say!"

"Is he?"

"Well, who else would he be, for heaven's sake?" Pinney's voice was very sharp.

He didn't act like one, very much, Alice thought. No hugs and kisses. But did Mr Scott dish out hugs and kisses? Alice wasn't sure if men did. It was a woman's province, perhaps. A mother's thing. Well, she had missed out on that and got used to it. A faint memory of her lovely dream came back, the woman holding out her arms and crying, "My Alice! My darling Alice!" It was the inflection on the "my" that she remembered. Whose Alice was she? Even Mrs Scott had felt more motherly than anyone she had known, and she had only met her the twice. Mr Ticino's Alice then, if Pinney said so, and much good that was when it came to hugs and kisses. Or nobody's Alice, if what that girl said was true.

"I don't look like him," she countered to Pinney.

"And thank goodness for that," Pinney said.

It was as funny as Mrs Pinney could manage, so Alice gave a polite laugh. Perhaps, before it had got thin and grey, Mr Ticino's hair had been thick and curly. She couldn't imagine it somehow.

"Perhaps I look like my mother."

"Yes, I daresay. She died when you were just a baby. I never knew her, dear."

And Mrs Pinney gave her a goodnight kiss, a very rare occurrence, usually only after the dentist or a bilious attack. It was like a hen pecking. Alice knew that Mrs Pinney knew she had cried at the party.

She took Goldie to bed with her and held him lovingly against her chest. He was rather hard and uncomfortable, but possessing him gave her a nice warm feeling. Goldie had done the trick with the wicked Snatchcorn. Goldie and Snatchcorn, her new friends. . . How could those people possibly think of killing Snatchcorn? She could not, would not, think about it, having shed too many tears today. It was too terrible. And that girl saying, "Mr Ticino's not her father."

So much for her happy day.

The next morning she ran out to Robin in the stable-yard. He knew all about her escapade with Snatchcorn.

"Everyone is talking about it. My brother told me. I

could've told you he was a killer, everyone knows it! They only keep him because he's sired a few good winners. Cor, I'd love to have seen it, you sitting in the manger chatting him up and all! Just like he was Daisy!"

"He was nice to me. More than that Ellen."

Alice told Robin about Goldie being thrown under the umbrella stand.

"Oh, that Miss Ellen, no one likes her," said Robin.

"Do you know all about Snatchcorn?"

"Of course I do. He belongs to Lord Falkenburg, and he was a very good racehorse. But wicked. And now everyone's frightened of him, although he's a good sire. I knew that Mr Scott wants to be rid of him."

"But Mr Scott doesn't own him! It's not for him to say. It's for Lord Falkenburg to say!"

"I suppose it is. But Lord Falkenburg doesn't have to look after him!"

"I could. I could look after him. He likes me."

"You'd better go and ask for a job then."

"What's Lord Falkenburg like?"

"He's all right. Youngish. The lads all like him because he's nice, not like some. Gives good tips, talks to them. Some of them nobility'll treat you like you're dirt."

Having sworn yesterday that she never wanted to set foot inside the Scott gates ever again, Alice now found that she couldn't think about anything else. She couldn't stop thinking about Snatchcorn, and how everyone had stared at her, sitting there with the killer. He did love her. She knew he did. The way his nostrils had quivered at her. That was a sign of love in a horse, like a dog wagging its tail. Perhaps if Lord Falkenburg saw how he was quiet with her he would not let him be destroyed. She longed to see Snatchcorn again.

"Could I call on Mrs Scott, and thank her for the party?" she asked Pinney.

"Well, that would be a bit forward. You should write a note."

"If I write a note, can I deliver it?"

"I don't see there would be any harm in that. The butler would take it."

"I'll make it my very best writing."

"Take a piece of Mr Ticino's paper. You want it nice."

"Yes. It will be perfect."

"And get the spelling right."

"Of course."

Alice wrote in her very best writing.

Dear Mrs Scott,
Thank you for having me to the party. It was very kind of you.

Useless to say how much she enjoyed it when she had wept so copiously into Mrs Scott's skirts.

I am sorry if I made a disturbance. I did not mean to upset anybody.

I hope it did not spoil it.
Yours sincerely,
Alice Ticino

She licked the envelope down so that Mrs Pinney couldn't read it, as she didn't know about the disturbance. Unless — as was very likely — she had heard the story on the Newmarket grapevine. No doubt Mabel had heard about it from her lad.

She took the letter in the afternoon, when she hoped she might meet William. Lessons generally finished at lunchtime. William had a tutor of his own, she knew, and was said to be very clever.

The place was quiet and only a couple of gardeners were in sight doing the herbaceous borders. Alice's feet crunched loudly on the gravel. She felt very nervous. Suppose the butler just took the letter and she didn't see anyone she knew? She wouldn't be able to think of another excuse to visit. She dreaded meeting horrid Ellen. Amelia wouldn't be so bad.

The front door was open but there were no sounds from inside.

Alice pulled the bell. It clanged loudly inside the house, and when the peel had finished, Alice could hear the thumping anticipation of her own heart. The thick white envelope was sticky with sweat. She prayed, "Please God, let it come right for me. Let it not be the butler! Not Ellen! Let it be William!"

And God, after all, was on her side. It was William.

"It's Alice!" He smiled.

She held out the letter, lost for words. William took it and tossed it carelessly on the hall table.

"Come to see Snatchcorn?"

Was he teasing? She said, in case he wasn't, "Can I?"

Perhaps the longing was evident in the two words, because he laughed and said, "Why not?"

And he came out on to the step and said, "See if you can work your magic again. Mr Anderson was telling Pa he ought to give you a job."

"Who's Mr Anderson?"

"The stud groom. The one in the bowler hat."

"He doesn't mean it!"

"Well, it's not possible, but if it were, yes, he means it. He's the one that has the responsibility. When the lad got injured – it's his fault really, that it happened. The boss always carries the can, doesn't he?"

Alice wasn't sure what he meant. He was strolling round the house with her, towards the small yard. Alice couldn't believe her luck. The power of prayer! "I will do anything for you, God, you are so kind to me!" Perhaps God was making up for her bad day at the the party. This was magic! William spoke to her as if he had known her for years, as if she were one of the family. And with him, she felt she was. He had a totally protective, kindly presence and gave her a feeling she had never experienced before. She had never had a proper friend, only the servants. How wonderful if William could be her friend!

Snatchcorn was looking over his half door. His ears were flat back on his head and the whites of his eyes showed in a thoroughly evil manner. Mr Anderson, the bowler hat man, was standing looking at him with a white-faced lad by his side.

"Your dear horse," William said to Alice.

It seemed no lad would take Snatchcorn on since his last one had been dispatched to hospital. William told Alice that his feed was just thrown in over the door and no one would muck him out.

Alice, well-versed in horse care by Tom and Robin, said, "That's cruel!"

Was God making up for all the dreadful experiences He had put her through lately? Had He especially timed her arrival at Snatchcorn's box for this very moment? Alice's heart brimmed with expectation.

"I'd rather not, sir, not even for double pay," the lad was saying.

William said, "Mr Anderson, you could give the job to Alice."

Mr Anderson spun round. He recognized Alice, she could tell, but disappointingly his face did not light up with joy. It did, however, gleam with a certain cunning.

"Well, miss, fancy. . ." His shrewd eyes flicked her up and down.

"I came to see Snatchcorn," Alice said boldly.

"You don't want to make friends with this one, miss. He's for the bullet when we can get a head collar on him."

Alice detected the uncertainty in his voice. She wanted to scream with anger at the man's words but took hold of herself firmly. She knew that God was on her side. She walked up to the stable door and held out her hand to Snatchcorn. She wasn't bold enough to go within range, but went close enough for him to reach out his head and sniff at her fingers.

Nobody said anything.

Alice watched the horse's face, and saw the same uncertainty as she knew she was showing.

It really did now depend on God.

She stepped over and put her arm up to stroke the horse's neck. She heard Mr Anderson make a sort of choking noise and the lad say, "Cor blimey!", but also she heard the softest snuffle of appreciation in the nostrils of the glorious stallion. She put all her trust in him not to bite her arm off, and he responded. His ears came up and he nuzzled gently at her hand. She found she was talking to him in her stupid Goldie voice, but this time she didn't care about it. He trusted her! Out of everyone in the whole world, it was only she he loved! Her face glowed. She heard William laughing.

Mr Anderson said gently, "Come away now, lass."

"I think you should clean his stable," Alice said as the smell wafted into her nostrils over the door.

They brought her a head collar and she put it on and led Snatchcorn out into the yard. By this time there were several lads standing by, all with pitchforks at the ready. But with Alice at his head the dreaded stallion showed no signs of his killer instinct.

"I find this hard to believe," Mr Anderson was saying.

A gang of lads cleaned the stable and filled it with fresh straw. But when it was ready for the horse to go back, Mr Anderson had a chain brought and the horse was chained to a ring in the wall. He could not look out of his door or move around.

"At least a lad will be able to get in and see to him without getting his head bitten off," he said.

"You can't keep him like that for ever!" Alice cried at him. "Not all the time!"

"There's no other way," Mr Anderson said tartly.

He did not seem particularly grateful to Alice for her intervention now the danger was over. He was sweating and looked as if he was in a state of shock.

"You showed 'em up, that's why," William said to her when everyone had dispersed. "And Anderson took a risk, letting you do that. My father would never have allowed it, I bet."

"Why not?"

"You're valuable, that's why."

"Who to? I've never noticed."

"Mr Ticino, I suppose." William looked embarrassed. "It would have been bad for the stable, wouldn't it? Little girl torn apart by horse. My father would have been furious."

Alice laughed. Then, said seriously, "They're not really going to shoot him, are they?"

"Well, you can see, it's pretty difficult looking after him. But he's a valuable horse, because he sires winners. So they would rather not shoot him. They keep putting it off, because his three-year-olds are running very well at the moment, and his value is going up all the time."

"I could come every day and look after him, so he doesn't have to be chained up."

"I don't think your father would allow it."

"Why not? It's not far. Ask your father to ask Mr Anderson."

"I don't think he would. It would mean admitting that none of them can do what a little girl can do. He wouldn't like it."

Alice could see the logic of this. Men were very proud.

"I'll ask him." He could only say no, after all.

Seeing the look on his face, she changed her tack. "Lord Falkenburg would like it. It's his horse. Surely he won't let them shoot him?"

"The horse is dangerous, Alice. He's killed someone. And nearly killed another." William was being very patient.

"Perhaps I could just come up every day, as if I were passing? Just looking in, pretend."

William laughed. "Why not?"

"I could write to Lord Falkenburg."

"Saying what?"

Alice considered. If she were Snatchcorn, what would she like? What made him so unhappy? Why did he hate everyone except her?

"He doesn't like it here. He would like a nice field, and some friends. And then he would be happy."

"Well, perhaps."

There were signs that William was getting bored with her. The day had gone better than she had ever dreamed; she must not outstay her welcome. Her insides were bounding with triumph.

But then . . . she had forgotten, momentarily. "You mustn't let them shoot him! They can't!"

"No, well, there's a colt that he sired running at Goodwood next week. And if he wins, I think Snatchcorn will get a reprieve. It's a very valuable race and the winner's sire will be in demand from all their Lordships, to see if they can breed one like it."

"What's he called, this colt?"

"Androcles."

"And if he doesn't win?"

William made a shooting sign at his temple. "Bang!"

Alice very carefully didn't scream or shout, but set off for home. Her head was reeling. All sorts of emotions – pride, excitement, fear, longing – swilled about in her brain so that she felt quite sick. Her head ached. She didn't know whether to laugh or cry.

"You've been a long time, miss!" Mrs Pinney said suspiciously.

"I was talking to William," she parried.

This seemed to set Pinney off.

"No harm in going to a party, but you don't want to get involved with that lot. It'll do you no good."

"Why not?"

"Because I say so!" The usual stupid answer, or non-answer.

"They're perfectly suitable."

"They are not suitable, madam, take my word for it."

"Why not?"

"You stick with Robin. He'll do you no harm, never mind he's daft and a servant."

Adults were so stupid, Alice thought crossly. How on earth could a smart family like the Scotts be branded unsuitable? Unsuitable meant common, dropping your aitches, or poor with holes in your shoes.

She went out again and told Robin about her experience. He knew all about Snatchcorn and Androcles. He was terribly impressed about her leading Snatchcorn out of the stable.

"You're kidding me!"

"No, you ask your brothers. I did it. Mr Anderson allowed me to."

"Blimey! Mr Scott wouldn't have, I bet! Of course, if Mr Scott saw that Snatchcorn was mucked out properly and chained up, Mr Anderson would get the credit. I bet he never told old Scotty it was down to you!"

"But chained up, Robin! It's cruel! How can they do it?"

"Or shoot him. What would you prefer?"

It was a terrible problem, and Alice couldn't get it out of

her head. Because Snatchcorn had showed his trust in her, she owed it to him to save him. He loved her.

But Mrs Pinney told Mr Ticino that Alice's head was full of the Scotts and William and a mad horse and that he must do something about it.

He forbade her to go to the Scotts again or to see William.

"Why?" Alice exploded. "They are nice people! The sort you like. Rich! Why can't I be friends with William?

"Because I say so."

"That's no answer! Tell me!"

"You will understand when you are older."

Mr Ticino looked out of his depth, beads of sweat standing on his forehead.

"Tell me!" screamed Alice.

"Mrs Pinney!" screamed Mr Ticino.

Mrs Pinney beat Alice on the bottom with one of Mr Ticino's slippers and locked her in her room. She got no supper, only a drink of water. Alice wept. She pretended she was Snatchcorn, chained to the wall for bad behaviour. She knew just how he felt! So bored, no jolly life to look forward to. No gallops and nice green grass, no rolling and running about. He was like her, chained to the likes of Miss Pratt and Sunday school and the thirteen times table.

"I love you, Snatchcorn. I will save you!"

But how? The next day Pinney told her she wasn't allowed out any more, only as far as the stable-yard and their little field to play with Robin, but not out of the gate. She poured out her woes to Robin. He didn't say anything, just looked a bit uncomfortable.

Androcles won his race by miles.

"They aren't going to shoot Snatchcorn – yet," Robin said.

"He might just as well be dead," Alice said.

He might be happier in God's bosom. Or in Horse Paradise. Except, with a temper like his, and being a murderer, he was bound to go to the Other Place.

Alice had no option but to forget her forays to the Scotts'. But the door that had opened in her life by going there had changed her perception of the future. She had no patience with it any longer, and threw her exercise books across the study.

"I want to go to school!" she roared.

She got slippered again.

She overheard Mrs Pinney say to Mr Ticino, "I don't know how long we can go on like this, sir. It'll all come out sooner or later; it's inevitable. I think you should see Lord—"

"Thank you, Mrs Pinney. When I want your advice I'll ask for it."

"It's not fair on the child, sir. She ought to go to school and mix with other children."

"You know perfectly well why she can't! You've said enough, Mrs Pinney."

"Yes, sir. But at least I've said it."

Whatever was that about? Alice turned it over and over in her head when she was in bed. It made no sense at all. She dared not ask. It paid her to behave herself these days, because she got fed up with being slippered and locked in her room with no supper. Mrs Pinney was in a permanent bad temper lately. Was it because of her? How could it be?

Alice talked to Goldie, and Goldie talked back to her in his horse voice: "Don't worry, Alice. Everything will be all right, in the end."

Perhaps.

Alice was eating her supper with Mr Ticino when there was a loud knocking on the front door. This was very unusual. They heard Mrs Pinney bustle along to answer it, and both stopped eating to listen to who it was.

"Mr Scott, sir," said Mrs Pinney. "He says it's urgent."

"Good gracious me!"

Mr Ticino shot to his feet and hurried out. Alice rushed after him but Mrs Pinney caught her by the arm.

"Not you, madam!"

But Mr Scott, standing in the hall, said in no uncertain tones, "Yes, it does concern Alice. That's what I've come about."

Mr Ticino went white as a sheet and said, "In private, surely?"

Mr Scott said, "It's another matter entirely, Mr Ticino, not what you are thinking. It's about my stallion, Snatchcorn. A most unfortunate thing has happened."

Mr Ticino then gave a nervous snort of laughter and said, "Oh, that!" in a very dismissive voice and looked all right again.

But Alice shouted, "What's happened? Is Snatchcorn all right?"

"Yes, certainly he's all right, but another party is far from all right. He's got a lad cornered in the box and is likely to kill him if we don't do something about it."

"How can he, when he's chained up?" Alice asked scornfully.

"He's broken the chain out of the wall. The lad was so terrified he jumped up onto the manger and into the rafters, and that's where he is now, with Snatchcorn below rearing up at him. We don't want to do any more violence than necessary, you understand, and Mr Anderson suggested sending for Alice, to see if she can work her magic."

"You're asking her to go to a killer horse!" Mr Ticino cried out.

"No. To entice him out. She's done it before. There will be no harm to her, I can assure you, Mr Ticino. Absolutely every precaution will be taken."

"This is the horse that belongs to Lord Falkenburg?"

"That's right."

"It's quite extraordinary," said Mr Ticino faintly. "Quite extraordinary. Wouldn't it be in order to send him a telegram first?"

"He's out of the country at the moment. I know that for a fact. Otherwise of course I would refer to him. It concerns him absolutely. But the boy can't hold on for ever – he's close to the hysterics as it is. It's a very fraught situation, otherwise I wouldn't be troubling you."

Mr Scott, Alice noticed, didn't treat Mr Ticino with the

respect he accorded to their graces and Lordships, but far more man to man, even tipping towards being the boss. His authority seemed to get to Mr Ticino, for he hesitated now.

Alice said, "Of course I can do it, Papa. Snatchcorn loves me."

"It sounds very dangerous."

"I can assure you, she will come to no harm."

Alice knew she had won.

"Go and fetch your coat then, and I will come with you. "Mr Scott's face lit up. "The carriage is outside. We'll be there in no time!"

Alice felt like the queen, entering the stable-yard behind the Scotts' mansion. Half the stable lads were assembled there, along with Mrs Scott and all her children and Mr Anderson in his bowler hat. They all fell back as the carriage spanked to a halt. Alice got down, very dignified, her heart pounding in her throat.

"Oh my Gawd!" said Mr Ticino.

Mr Scott led Alice up to the open half-door of Snatchcorn's box. Alice looked in. She laughed.

Seated astride the rafters, just out of the horse's reach, a large spotty-faced lad looked down on her with tears of fright oozing from his eyes. He was in a precarious position, holding on with one hand to a cross-beam, but depending mainly on his balance not to fall down. Snatchcorn stood immediately below him, covered with lather, switching his tail. His ears were flat back on his head. He looked, even to Alice, very evil.

Her confidence dipped a fraction, but determination quashed the blip.

"Snatchcorn!" she called.

Did her voice quaver?

Snatchcorn took no notice, but stamped a hoof.

"Get rid of all these bystanders," Mr Scott said to Anderson. "Clear the yard. Fetch my gun."

"Snatchcorn," Alice prattled. "Come and talk to me. You are so beautiful and I love you. Come and see me."

One ear went back and wavered in her direction. Alice forgot about everything else. She leaned confidentially over the door and started talking. She talked about his friend Goldie and the weather and how clever his son Androcles was winning at Goodwood and wouldn't he like to have lots more sons like that and not get shot?

Snatchcorn turned his head and looked at her.

Alice pulled back the bolt and opened the door.

"Come and talk to me. I've left my supper to come and see you, so you can't go on bullying that poor boy. He wants his supper too and you are just being stupid."

"Steady on," said Mr Scott.

He put a hand on her shoulder. Alice shook it off.

"He's coming," she said.

Both ears were forward now, not just the one. The head remained turned towards her. Who was this idiot, the horse was thinking, interrupting his games?

"Alice," said Alice. "Your friend. Come on, you big elephant."

Mr Scott pressed a carrot into her hand. His hand shook.

Alice was waiting for the feet to move. The horse still had his back to the door.

He had to come round. Only his head was turned towards her. She told Mr Scott to go away. Mr Scott retreated and Mr Anderson handed him a gun.

"Come on," said Alice. "If you come right round you can have this carrot. Otherwise I shall take it home to Goldie and Goldie will eat it. He's not stupid like you. He likes carrots and he doesn't terrify stable lads. When he dies he'll go to Heaven, which is more than you will do. If you don't pull your socks up a frightful fate will befall you, and then you'll be sorry. You'll be sorry you were such a bully boy. Come on now. Carrots! Yum yum."

She took a bite herself.

Snatchcorn turned round. He reached out his head and his lips gobbled towards the carrot.

"Come a bit nearer," Alice said.

The horse took a pace forward.

Alice gave him the carrot. "Yummy yum yum," said Alice. "Give me a head collar."

Mr Scott held one out.

Alice took a step forward and stroked Snatchcorn's nose. He nuzzled at her kindly now and Alice put her hand up behind his head and stroked his neck. The horse made no move to step back. Alice took the head collar and reached up to put it over the horse's nose.

"Can you reach?" Mr Scott breathed.

"Bring your head down a bit, you big elephant," Alice commanded the horse.

By standing on tiptoe she could pass the head collar strap over behind the horse's ears. Snatchcorn did not resist. Alice did up the buckle.

"There. You are a good boy. A very good boy."

Snatchcorn got another carrot.

Then Alice led him out of the stable into the yard. He followed her like a pet dog.

The boy flumped down into the straw and burst into loud blubbing and Mrs Scott came out and took him in hand. Mr Anderson had taken off his bowler hat and was mopping his brow, the lads were all goggling round the corner of the gateway and Mr Scott was grinning all over his face.

"Thank God! Thank God! You are a miracle, Alice!"

He put his arm round her shoulders, and Snatchcorn's ears went back and he made a lunge for him with teeth bared. Mr Scott stepped hastily back. Alice jerked on the head collar and said, "Naughty boy!"

Snatchcorn's ears went forward again. Alice's stroked his neck kindly.

The family had returned from their retreat beyond the gate, and William came up grinning and said, "You are a nut, Alice. I think Pa will have to employ you here."

Alice glanced up and saw Ellen watching her with a strange, jealous gleam in her eyes.

"She's like a gypsy," she said. "She hypnotizes him."

"What a weird thing to say!" William jeered. "A gypsy! I bet you couldn't have done it! She's brave," he said staunchly.

"She is indeed," said Mr Scott. "By Jove, that's a great relief. You have a magic in you, Alice, like the old horse whisperers. I've known it before, but it's rare, believe me."

"What are you going to do with him now?"

"I'm going to send a wire to Lord Falkenburg and ask him to remove the horse from my stables. I can't have any more of this. It's all too dangerous."

"What will he do with him?"

"It's for him to decide. It's not my responsibility."

Alice thought, *Perhaps he will give him to me. I can take him home and put him next to Daisy.*

She said, "You mustn't chain him up again. It's cruel."

"Well, perhaps. The sooner he goes away from here the better."

The boys cleaned out the stable and put feed in, and Alice led Snatchcorn back in. Then Mr Scott asked Mr Ticino to come indoors for a drink and Alice went too. The adults went into the study and Alice was left with William and Ellen and Amelia.

"Why don't you come here any more?" Amelia asked.

"My father won't let me."

"Why not?"

Alice looked at Ellen and said, "He thinks you're unsuitable for me."

"He's like Queen Victoria, disapproves of racing," said Amelia comfortably. "He looks a bit like her, doesn't he? Not so fat. If he had a bun and a crown. . ."

"He doesn't! And he doesn't disapprove of racing. It's all he thinks about, betting on the horses."

"That's why he's so poor," Ellen said contemptuously.

Alice had heard Mrs Pinney on this subject and knew it was true so did not argue.

"Our father never bets," Ellen said.

"His whole life is a gamble, trying to keep their Lordships happy," William said, and laughed.

William was so nice, Alice thought, and Ellen so truly horrible – one could never believe they were brother and sister. Ellen seemed determined to hate her.

"They're talking about you coming to live here," Amelia said.

"Amelia!" Both William and Ellen let out a roar of horror and Amelia went bright red and clapped her hand to her face.

"Oh, I shouldn't have said that!"

"Come and live here?" Alice felt the floor had suddenly dropped from beneath her feet. "This isn't my home!"

William and Ellen both gaped at her, unable to think of anything to say to cover up Amelia's indiscretion. Whatever did they know that she didn't? That Mr Ticino wasn't her father?!

Alice let out a wail. "Who am I?"

"Oh, come on, Alice," said William, acutely embarrassed.

"Don't be daft. No one can make you do what you don't want to do. It's a only a stupid idea."

"Why?"

William groped for an answer, and gave up. "I can't tell you."

"You could look after Snatchcorn," Amelia said, trying to help.

"I want to go home!" Alice sobbed.

The study door opened and Mrs Scott looked out.

"What's wrong? Alice, dear, whatever's the matter?"

"I don't want to live here!" Alice wailed.

"Oh, my dear, whatever have these silly children been saying?" She came out and put an arm round Alice. "Come in the kitchen, dear, and I'll give you a nice cocoa and a biscuit."

She gave Ellen and William a terrible glare and said, "Go to your rooms at once! You've been very silly."

"It was Amelia," Ellen sneaked.

"Go!"

She was worse than Mrs Pinney, Alice thought wildly. But in the kitchen she was kind. Alice's brain felt bruised by all the uncertainties that were shaking it.

"Why isn't Mr Ticino my father? I heard them say at the party—"

"Hush, dear. Mr Ticino is very good to you. You know him as your father. Nothing is any different."

Then she said, "But it's not right that you should live with him in that house without any other children to play with, and he doesn't let you go to school. We are just discussing how to make your life happier, Alice. You are such a brave little girl."

"I want to go to school," said Alice. But what business was it of Mrs Scott's? Alice, calmed by cocoa and gingerbread, did not like to ask.

"Yes, and make friends. I think you should. It's your welfare we are discussing, Alice, so don't be afraid. Your future."

And that was all she would say. Alice was left more confused than ever.

A groom drove her home, with Mr Ticino sitting pale and despondent at her side. He would not answer her tentative questions, but just said, "Wait and see."

"Wait how long?"

"Not long. Not long at all."

Alice told Mrs Pinney what had happened and asked her why.

"WHY were they talking about me in the study?"

"Go to bed," said Mrs Pinney. "And don't be a silly girl."

So Alice went to bed. But she couldn't sleep for wondering what was going to happen to her. And who she was.

"Your name is Alice Not-Ticino," Goldie said to her, "And nobody knows who you are. Nobody!"

He was hard and cold in her embrace, but he was all she had. Alice wept some more.

Chapter Five

When she awoke, Alice decided she could not go through another day without knowing what everyone else knew: who her father was. Nobody would tell her. But Robin knew; he would tell her.

"I can't," he said.

"Why not?"

"My father'll beat the hide off me."

"He needn't know! I won't tell who told me. I needn't even show that I know! I can keep mum, like a mouse."

She had cornered Robin in the stable, where he was giving Daisy her midday feed.

"Some mouse!" said Robin. "I can't see you keeping quiet."

"Why not? Is it so amazing?"

"Yes," said Robin.

At this, Alice realized she would die if she didn't find out. Whatever would make Robin tell her something worth getting a belting for?

"Now they like me at the Scotts', I might be able to get you a job there," she tried.

"Huh," said Robin.

"If you tell me, I'll see to it. Mr Anderson relies on me."
She didn't think it very tactful to suggest that there was a job
going looking after Snatchcorn.

"I bet," said Robin scornfully.

But he looked thoughtful.

Alice pressed her cause. "If everybody in Newmarket
knows, surely I should know? I could go up the high street and
ask anybody, couldn't I? That's what I'll do. I'll go and ask in
the Rutland Arms."

"You wouldn't dare."

No, she wouldn't, but she didn't have to admit it.

"I'll get you a job."

She could see that this tempted Robin.

He didn't say anything. Then: "If I tell you, will you promise
not to say it was me? Say you heard it, in the street. Someone
talking."

"Yes!"

She waited.

Robin looked anguished. "I can't!"

"You can!"

Robin screwed himself into the corner of Daisy's stall,
hopping from foot to foot.

"Promise you won't say it was me?"

"Promise. Cross my heart and hope to die!"

"Your father is the owner of Snatchcorn, Lord Falkenburg.
And William is your twin brother."

Alice wasn't sure she heard this properly. Her mouth

72

dropped open and she gazed at Robin with eyes that seemed to tremble. Then they turned up into her head and she dropped at his feet in a dead faint.

"Oh my God!"

Robin nearly passed out too, his heart bucketing with fright at what he had done. Daisy put her nose down and gave the tumbled body a questioning push.

"Alice, you idiot! Alice! Alice!"

He put the feed scoop in Daisy's water bucket and threw a scoopful of water over Alice's head. Apart from soaking her it had no effect. Robin thought she had died of fright. He went to run for Mrs Pinney, thought of the secret he had revealed and stopped short in the doorway. His father, just coming back from a morning's gardening, saw his consternation and said, "What's got into you?"

"It's Alice."

Tom came to look.

"Why . . . whatever. . .? Is she ill?"

"She wanted to know who her father is, so I told her."

Not a good move. With a roar his father lifted Robin clean off his feet, threw him across the feed bin and started strapping him with the handle-end of Mr Ticino's driving whip.

Tom bellowed and screamed to such effect that Mrs Pinney and Mabel came running down the garden to see what was going on.

"Oh my Gawd!" shrieked Mrs Pinney, seeing Alice. "Whatever's happened?"

"Leave that poor boy be!" Mabel shouted at Tom.

Alice, face down in the straw, heard all the shrieking and thought the end of her world had happened. Such shouting and screaming. Mrs Pinney's face coming and going. "My poor lamb! What's wrong?"

Tom told Mrs Pinney and Mrs Pinney started screaming at Robin, and Tom started back again with the whip handle. Mabel got down in the straw with Alice.

"He said Lord Falkenburg," whispered Alice.

"Yes, aren't you a lucky girl? Much better than Mr Ticino." She stroked Alice's soaking hair. "They wouldn't tell you without his permission, and he's abroad somewhere. That's why they kept putting you off. I said to tell you all along. But such a shock, my poor duck."

"Why . . . why?" But Alice felt too peculiar to talk. She could hear Robin sobbing his heart out. All her fault! Tom and Mrs Pinney were arguing. Mabel helped her sit up. Daisy moved over obligingly and gave her another shove with her nose. Alice couldn't help a giggle.

"Am I a lady?"

Mabel snorted. "Some lady! No, my duck, you're just another little bastard. The world's full of 'em."

At this Mrs Pinney, having finished her row with Tom, struck Mabel a sharp blow round the ears, crying out, "Hold your tongue, you ignorant girl! How dare you use such words in front of our little lamb!"

Mabel got up and retorted angrily, "It's true! Say it isn't, I dare you! The poor little thing, treated like a parcel, to cover up some scandal in the Marlborough set – I wonder Robin didn't tell her that her pa is the Prince of Wales! Could just as easily have been——"

"Hold your tongue!" roared Mrs Pinney again.

Alice staggered to her feet. The stable floated round her head and in the clouds she saw William's face coming and going, her brother. Her twin brother! Half of her, half herself. No wonder she had had this feeling of knowing him. She did know him! But – unlike herself – he was so wise, so cool, so altogether! That was his drawing-room upbringing, as opposed to her kitchen upbringing. How she loved him, her own! She was somebody after all. She was William's twin sister.

She was then very sick in Daisy's straw, and Mrs Pinney gathered her to her stringy bosom and said, "You must go to bed and rest, and I'll give you some powders. The shock is too much for you. That stupid boy. . ." A great glare at poor Robin. Robin was still howling and rubbing his beaten bottom.

"It wasn't his fault – I made him say!" Alice lamented.

"The lad knows what's what. He had no excuse!"

Mabel said staunchly, "It's a good thing the wretched business is out in the open. It should have been discussed with the Scotts and her father long ago."

For this she got another whack round the ears from Mrs Pinney, but she dodged nicely. She was red with indignation, and put her arm consolingly round Robin's shoulders.

"You did right, young Robin. Take no notice of them!"

Flagrantly on Alice's side, her annoyance rather threw Mrs Pinney, who sniffed angrily and said, "Well, it'll make for changes, mark my words. And where will that leave us, you stupid girl?"

"I don't care! It's for Alice's good."

And Alice was sent to bed with a dose of one of Mrs Pinney's standby potions, to lie dreaming in the sunbeams that played on her pillow. Her mind, she felt, was out of her body, up with the sun, bursting with its new knowledge. Mr Ticino was only her keeper after all, no part of her at all. Her father was the mythical Lord Falkenburg whose name was well-known in Newmarket – a toff, owner of Snatchcorn. Did that make Snatchcorn hers? Did it make her a lady? She was a lady! *Oh, William, my brother!* Her head ached and reeled and soon she was sick again, all over the sheets. Mrs Pinney was annoyed although she tried not to show it.

"That Robin!" she fumed.

"What is going to happen?" Alice whispered.

"Gawd knows."

What happened was that Mr Ticino came home and learned that his secret was out. He wasn't actually sick like Alice but certainly looked it. Alice heard him say, "We'd better get in touch with the Scotts and tell them what's happened. Then they can raise Lord Falkenburg, wherever he is. He's responsible, after all."

"Shall I send a message round, sir?" Mrs Pinney asked.

"Yes. Send Robin. Or Mabel if you can't find him."

"Yes, sir. Would you like your supper first, sir, before the balloon goes up?"

"Yes, I think so."

Alice came down and had chicken broth with Mr Ticino. She was very pale and had no words to say to him. *Not my father*, she was thinking. The relief was overwhelming. She felt the strength creeping back into her. She felt that she must keep the lid on her head, or she would fly off into outer space. A father, a brother and the heavenly Snatchcorn, all hers in the space of a few hours . . . it was beyond her capacity to feel calm. But she tried.

Mr Ticino said, "I hear Robin's been spilling the beans?"

"Yes."

"Well, it had to be, sooner or later. Ever since your escapade on the heath, delivering yourself into the Scott family, it was bound to happen this way. I was hoping it could wait until Lord Falkenburg comes back, but now we've rather jumped the gun. Never mind."

After the first shock, he seemed to be taking it quite calmly. "It had to be."

"What will happen?"

"That will depend on Lord Falkenburg."

"Will I go away?"

"Probably. I am not considered a fit keeper for you any longer."

It didn't seem to worry him now that he had got used to the idea.

"Your father paid me, you see, and I have come to rely on the money rather. When my wife was alive, it was a very good arrangement, but since she died it has gradually become untenable."

Alice stared. "Was your wife my mother?"

"Good heavens no! What an idea!" Mr Ticino was plainly shocked.

"I don't understand!"

"Oh dear. No. Let me explain. I was hoping to leave all this to Mrs Scott. Oh dear. Of course you want to know. . ."

He was flustered now, never having expended so many words on Alice in his life before. "Mrs Scott will tell you everything. But, basically, it was like this. Lord Falkenburg comes here often to see his racehorses. And when he had you two twin children he thought it was a good idea if he lodged you with the Scotts so that when he came to see his racehorses he could see you two as well."

"But why did he give us away? Why didn't his wife keep us?"

Mr Ticino went bright red.

He said, "I would really rather leave this to Mrs Scott."

"Our mother gave us away!"

"Yes, that's a fact. But it was impossible for her to keep you. Quite impossible. Don't ask me why. Ask Mrs Scott. It was not because she didn't love you and want you. It was circumstances."

Mr Ticino's face glistened with sweat and he was still red and very uncomfortable. There were still secrets there, Alice could see.

"But Mrs Scott only wanted William?" she prompted.

"Mrs Scott had just had Amelia. She had an older girl already and one more baby, as well as Amelia, was all she could cope with. Mr Scott wanted the boy, so they just took William and my wife took you. My wife was a very good friend of Mrs Scott's. We all thought it the best arrangement possible. But when you were two my dear wife died, and at the same time I fell out with Mr Scott over a business arrangement, a building venture, so the obvious course of handing you over to Mrs Scott then rather went by the board."

Mr Ticino mopped his sweating face with his napkin and sighed deeply. Alice had never heard him talk like this before. But it was only half the story.

"Who is our mother then?"

"I don't know, Alice, and that is the truth."

"Did Mrs Ticino know? Does Mrs Scott know?"

"No, certainly not Mrs Ticino. Mrs Scott – I don't know. As far as I know, only Lord Falkenburg knows."

Alice thought, *Gossip must know! Mrs Pinney must know!*

But when she asked her, after supper, Mrs Pinney said, "My Gawd, if I knew that, I'd know the best-kept – the only – secret in Newmarket! Nobody knows who your mother is, my chicken. You'll have to make do with knowing who your father is, for the time being."

"I've never seen him. Have you?"

"Yes, I have."

"What's he like?"

79

"He's gorgeous!" said Mabel. "So handsome, and such a gentleman. Oh, but you're a lucky one, to have such a father! It's a crime you thinking Mr Ticino was your father all this time—"

"Hold your tongue!" Mrs Pinney bellowed. "Such things you're saying! Mr Ticino's done his best by her, poor gentleman, and I don't know how you can regard his Lordship so highly after the way he's behaved by the two mites."

"Giving us away, you mean?"

Mrs Pinney made her *harrumph* noise, which Alice knew boded danger, so she kept quiet. Her head was still spinning with all it knew already. Adding a mother too would finish her. Robin brought a message from Mrs Scott saying she would be round in the morning to discuss the situation with Mr Ticino and would he kindly be in at ten o'clock. Alice went to bed and dreamed she was a princess and lay in a bedroom full of flowers with peacocks shrilling on the lawns outside and a flunky in silk stockings pulling her curtains open to a sunny morning. But it was only Mabel pulling her curtains to a wet windy day, and the grey and brown roses still drearily adorned the walls and the brown linoleum was as cold to her feet as ever.

"What is going to happen?" she whispered to Mabel.

"I reckon Mrs Scott'll take you," Mabel said.

The prospect both thrilled and appalled Alice. She lay thinking about it. Being with William would be all right, but Ellen . . . ugh! She hated Ellen! And what about Robin? And

Mabel? Suddenly her boring life with Mr Ticino seemed far more desirable than it usually did. Even lessons with Miss Pratt were suddenly quite attractive. Suppose she had to share lessons with Ellen? Or – horrors! – a bedroom! She had never been anywhere but in this now suddenly quite attractive house with dear Mabel and kind Mrs Pinney. To live with the Scotts . . . with William. And Snatchcorn. Snatchcorn! Maybe she could call him hers. Nobody else seemed to want him. Save her father.

Her father! A lordship. All this time she had never known. How her head was whirling!

Mrs Scott arrived on her own two feet on the dot of ten. She spoke with Mr Ticino for half an hour in the morning room and then Alice was called in.

"We don't want to keep you in the dark, Alice," Mrs Scott said. "This has been a great shock to you and you need to know what is going to happen. Your father, Lord Falkenburg, is at this moment on his way back from America and should arrive in London some time next week. We have sent word to him to come up to Newmarket at once, so you will meet him very soon. Until then, I would like you to come and live with us."

She looked slightly worried, not sure if Alice was going to burst into loud tears at the thought. But Alice stayed very calm. She had guessed, after all. It surely must be better there than here with Mr Ticino? "It's only just a little way away, dear. You can always come back and visit Mr Ticino whenever you like," Mrs Scott said kindly.

Alice was thinking more of Mrs Pinney, Mabel, Robin and Tom than Mr Ticino. She wouldn't dare say so, though. She was now a lady!

She nodded. "Yes." Her voice sounded very small.

So it was going to happen.

"When?" she whispered.

"Whenever you like, dear. When Mrs Pinney has packed your things together." What things? Her clothes would go in one suitcase and her only other thing was Goldie. Her improving books she would leave behind. But Mabel . . . and Robin. . .

"Can . . . can Mabel come?"

Mrs Scott looked surprised.

Mr Ticino said hastily, "Certainly not, Alice! You're much too young to have a maid of your own."

Then Mrs Scott said, slightly doubtfully, "Possibly I could employ Mabel in the kitchen. I can understand the child wanting a familiar face by her. But that would be depriving you."

Mr Ticino looked miffed, and Alice thought he was more upset at the thought of losing Mabel than of losing her. But why not, after all? Mabel was useful to him.

Mrs Scott said tactfully, "We can discuss it later, perhaps. We're so close, Alice – you can always run round and see your friends."

Alice knew that her new prospects were exciting. She was going up in the world. But she was frightened, all the same. The best thing to think of was William, her brother. And

Snatchcorn. Snatchcorn would be just round the corner: her horse. Yes, she would go. She would love it.

"Yes. If I pack my things can I come back with you?"

Mrs Scott was taken by surprise, but agreed.

Mr Ticino said, "My man can bring her suitcase round later."

His man would turn out to be Robin, Alice guessed, and she would be able to show him Snatchcorn. Better and better. She jumped to her feet eagerly.

Mrs Scott laughed. "Well, no time like the present!"

Alice went down to the kitchen and gave the news. To her amazement Mrs Pinney wept. She clasped Alice to her bony frame and said, "My poor little duck, you just come straight back if you don't like it."

Mabel looked gloomy and said, "It'll be quiet without you and no mistake."

Alice thought they would be relieved to be rid of her. How surprising! She didn't know what to say. Better not to mention that Mrs Scott might give Mabel a job. Mabel might not want a change.

Mr Ticino showed Mrs Scott out of the front door. Alice never used the front door and hardly knew the front of the house she was now leaving. Mr Ticino gave her a peck on the forehead and said, "Be a good girl now, Alice," but looked far from tears. He was a remarkably expressionless man, Alice realized, and looked much the same whether his bets came up and he won, or whether the horse came in last and he lost a week's salary. Losing Alice was only a small and unremarkable bet to him. Mrs Ticino couldn't have had much fun with him.

"What was Mrs Ticino like?" she asked Mrs Scott as they set off down the road.

"Oh, she was a dear, a poor dear girl. She was an orphan and had a very hard life, brought up by an aunt, her only relative. And when the aunt died she was left almost destitute, and married Mr Ticino, the first man to ask her, to get a roof over her head. I met her in church and we became friends. She jumped at the chance of taking you, when it arose, as she so wanted a child. It seemed a perfect solution, my taking William and dear Rose taking you. We saw so much of each other, you see, and as babies you two were together a lot of the time. But then she died very suddenly of cholera and, strangely I thought, Mr Ticino insisted on keeping you. He was well paid for it, of course, by Lord Falkenburg, which was the main reason, and I suppose he loved Rose in his way, and wanted a reminder of her, even though you weren't really their child. He employed Mrs Pinney, looked after you like a mother, so no harm was done. But he did not keep up any relationship with our family, and although I called several times I found it very difficult to have any conversation with him, and after a while – seeing that you were so well looked after by Mrs Pinney – I stopped calling. But I always thought it wrong that you were parted from William. So when you arrived in our midst on that bolting horse it seemed to me like an intervention from Heaven. I said then that you should come

84

back to us, but oh – men! Mr Ticino didn't want it, my husband said you were perfectly all right where you were, Lord Falkenburg wasn't anywhere to be found . . . they have no idea about children! So it has taken me quite a while to sort it out. I always wanted you in our family. It's where you belong."

Was it? Alice wasn't sure at all. Surely she and William belonged to Lord Falkenburg's wife, their mother, whoever she was? Presumably she was dead, or they wouldn't have been given away. But that was too much to be thinking of for now. The story of Mrs Ticino was enough for the moment and she asked no more questions, thinking about it. She supposed Mrs Scott was now her mother, which was fairly agreeable. Mrs Scott wasn't a great one for hugging and spoiling and lying on the sofa giving out bonbons (Alice's idea of a real mother), but she was a straightforward sort of woman, the sort you could go to, not frightening. Her husband seemed to be rather bad-tempered, what she had seen of him – which wasn't much – but Alice thought that was probably because of the worries of his job, not to do with his family. It was no joke training valuable racehorses for rich owners, as everyone in Newmarket knew. Most good trainers were fierce to people, although nice to their horses.

The only question she asked was, "When is Lord Falkenburg coming back?"

"He's on his way now."

It was a hot August day. Walking up the gravelled drive Alice gave a little skip at the thought that this was now her home. She felt both excited and slightly sick, although everything was perfectly calm – no welcoming committee, nobody at all, only the manservant Charles taking Mrs Scott's parasol.

"The children are out visiting today. They've gone to the MacIntyres' on their ponies," Mrs Scott said.

Would this be her lot too, to visit the MacIntyres' on a pony? Or would she be the poor relation, left at home? No pony. No invitation. Her stomach churned.

"Maybe we can find a place for your things, and see where you can sleep. Ellen's room is very big and there would be plenty of space for another bed there."

Oh no! Alice thought.

"On the other hand, you might prefer to be on your own."

"Oh yes please! I'd rather," she said. Then tactfully, "I don't want to disturb Ellen." The house seemed huge to Alice, yet all the rooms on the second floor were taken as bedrooms, a best guest room, playrooms and sewing and ironing rooms, and Mrs Scott doubtfully took Alice up what she called the maids' stairs.

"The servants' quarters are on the top floor, but none of our servants live in so the rooms are all spare. William has a study in one of them, and some are full of lumber, but there is a nice one empty at the end. You might like it."

She opened a door and Alice saw a dormer window directly opposite which looked straight into the home stable-yard. Snatchcorn's box was directly opposite!

"Oh, it's lovely! Yes, I would love to have this room! Please!"

"It's rather small." Mrs Scott could not see the attraction.

But Alice thought it was perfect, tucked under the eaves with a sloping roof and the entrancing view to hand. If she had the bed in the right place she would be able to see Snatchcorn from her bed. She would put Goldie in the window sill so that he could look out and talk to Snatchcorn.

"You won't be lonely up here?"

"No!"

"All right then. I'll get some more furniture brought up, and a nice carpet. Charles will do it now and you can sleep in it tonight. But if you don't like it we'll make the ironing room over for you."

So much to think about! What if Mabel came and had a room on the top floor too? What larks! And Robin could get a job in the stable-yard . . . and Tom. . .

Mrs Scott said, "I'll take you into Cambridge and get you some new clothes. You must look nice for his Lordship coming home."

New clothes! And what about a pony, Alice thought, like the others, to go visiting on? Some girls her age had their own pony and trap. You saw them about. Perhaps his Lordship. . .?

Mabel staggered round with Alice's suitcase later and Alice showed her the room and told her all her plans.

"Would you like to come here?"

"Yes, I would, but the work would be hard in a place like

this. Doing for such a big family – all that carrying hot water upstairs and doing the fires. They keep you at it from dawn till dusk, these sort of people. It's very boring with Mr Ticino, but very easy. I know when I'm well off. But I might get the sack now you've gone, so we'll see what happens."

"You could fall in love with a stable lad and get married. There's hundreds of them out there."

"Yes, well, you know I've got my eye on one already." Mabel laughed. "Might get a better one here, though!"

After she had departed, the Scott children came home from the MacIntyres'. Alice heard the clatter of hooves in the home stable-yard, and felt her sick feeling come back. She would be a surprise to them, already ensconced. She dreaded Ellen, but worse was the fear that William might not want her underfoot. He was quite an alone sort of person, she knew. She could not bear for William to resent her.

But her fears on that score were unfounded. In his calm way, he smiled with real pleasure to hear that she had come for good. It wasn't just politeness, she could see. Amelia was thrilled and danced around Alice, pulling her hand to come and see her new pony, and the other little girls, Jemima and Grace, bundled up to her like enthusiastic puppies, wanting to know if she was William's sister was she their sister too?

But Ellen's face was like thunder. She flung down her riding crop and said, "I hope she's not sharing a room with me!"

Mrs Scott said calmly, "No. That wouldn't be a good idea."

"I don't want her here!"

"Ellen, manners!"

Ellen flung out of the room, slamming the door behind her. Alice, convinced she didn't care, for she hated Ellen, found she cared terribly. It was like being slapped in the face. William said immediately, "Don't take any notice of her. She's like that. She can't help it."

"It's her age," said Mrs Scott apologetically. "I'm sorry, Alice. It's not just you – she can be very difficult. I try not to get too angry with her; it just makes her worse. She has a very jealous nature, I'm afraid."

"She's like it with me," William comforted Alice. "Cuckoo in the nest. Two cuckoos now. She thinks she'll get pushed out."

"Oh really, William!" Mrs Scott laughed. "Let's hope she mends her manners when Ralph comes."

"Who's Ralph?" Alice asked. Not another brother?!

"Lord Falkenburg, dear. His name's Ralph. Why don't you show William your room before tea? He might find some books for you, or a picture or two. It looks rather bare still."

Thank goodness, to be alone with William! Alice flumped on her new bed. William looked out of the window and laughed.

"I can see why you wanted this one! You can talk to Snatchcorn all night."

"He can't look out chained up like that. As soon as Lord Falkenburg – Ralph – my father – comes home I'm going to get him to see to it. You can't keep a horse like that."

"No. Mr Scott can't wait to be rid of him. You two can work it out together, what to do with him. You've arrived just at the right time."

"What's he like, Lord Falkenburg?"

"Oh, he's nice. Not a bit stuffy, not stuck up. He doesn't expect to be waited on, like some of the toffs."

"Is he old?"

"Not at all. Quite young to have us, about thirty-five, I think. He dashes about – he's a great rider, and plays tennis and all those things. You'll really like him."

Promising, Alice thought. Now she was alone with William she thought it was time to ask the obvious question.

"Who is our mother?"

William scowled. "I don't know," he said.

"Have you asked?"

"Yes, and he won't say anything. He just says he can't tell me, and that's it. Nobody knows who our mother is, not Mrs Scott or anybody."

Alice thought it very odd – she had assumed that William would know. But as she had so many new people to absorb, she wasn't sorry for the time being. Mrs Ticino, deceased, would do for now. She sounded really nice and Mrs Scott had loved her. It was amazing how much better that made her feel about things.

William said, "I might as well point out to you, before Ellen does, that our father wasn't married to our mother. Our father has never been married."

Alice thought you had to be married to have children. She couldn't work this out. "What do you mean?"

"It means we are illegitimate."

"Whatever's that?"

"It means the children of two people born out of wedlock. It's scandalous to be illegitimate. I don't mind being a scandal but you might. I'm just warning you. People make nasty remarks. Ellen will, I bet, when her mother isn't around. I think that's why Mr Ticino wouldn't let you go to school, because he knew the other girls would make nasty remarks. He was trying to protect you, keeping you in ignorance of who you are."

"So who am I?" Alice didn't understand.

"You are the illegitimate child of Lord Falkenburg. So am I. At least he's a lord, which helps a bit. People respect lords, even if they're scandalous."

Alice found it very confusing. She didn't know about these things. She didn't like to show how ignorant she was to William, although he seemed to know. She would ask Mabel about it later. Mabel was much informed about scandal.

"Don't worry about it," William said. "I just thought you should know. Mrs Scott probably won't tell you and Ellen might get it in first."

"I don't like Ellen."

"Nor do I. But don't take any notice of her. She'll say some very nasty things to you, I bet, but just ignore her."

"What's wrong with her?"

91

William shrugged. "It's just the way she is."

"She doesn't like me coming here."

"No."

William hesitated. Not an emotional boy, he then managed to add, "But I do. I'm glad you're here. You should have been here all the time." His assurance was all Alice needed. Her heart filled with an unaccustomed surge of loving: what for, exactly, she wasn't sure. Certainly for William, but also for the sad Rose, her one-time mother, and for the staunch and kindly Mrs Scott, and for the dashing Ralph, yet to be made known. And Mrs Pinney. That made three mothers – of a sort – so far.

And that left the star part – that of her real mother – as unfulfilled as ever, the eternal mystery. When William departed she lay on her bed, staring at the ceiling, thinking about it.

Chapter Six

"He's come up on the train. His own horses are up from London and are meeting him at the station. He'll be here in five minutes."

Alice was already washed, brushed and in her new nicest dress, waiting. She wore her hair loose now, every day (it was rather hot and took some getting used to). She had discovered that she seemed to have grown up in the last few days, since arriving at the Scotts'. She was no longer chivvied by Mrs Pinney. She hadn't realized before just how chivvied she had been. Mrs Scott treated her almost like a grown-up, so it made her behave like one. Very interesting. She tried to pretend she was quite calm about meeting Lord Falkenburg. Maybe it worked on the outside, just standing in the hall waiting for the crunch of hooves on the gravel, but inside her heart was churning with excitement and a sweat of fear prickled round her lace collar. William, of course was unconcerned.

"He's not a bit lordy," he said.

Not unexpectedly, Lord Falkenburg had the most beautiful pair of carriage horses Alice had ever seen. As they came up the drive Alice's fears were distracted by admiration of the snow-white pair, stepping in perfect unison.

"It means he's going to stay a bit, if he brings his horses," William said to Alice.

His horses were beautiful! But she tore her eyes away to focus on the figure who was jumping down without waiting for a man to open the door. He didn't look like a father at all: so young and agile, not pompous, no whiskers, but a rather untidy head of dark red-brown curls and quick, matching eyes. His skin was pale and faintly freckled, the nose the most lordy feature about him, very straight and imperious like the Duke of Wellington's. But his manner was open, unaffected and reassuringly cheerful. After all, Alice thought afterwards, he must have been slightly worried about meeting her, in case she was weedy and pimply and knock-kneed. But when he smiled so engagingly at her, she lifted her head and radiated relief, her smile bursting out.

"Father!"

"My dear Alice! How lovely to meet you at last! All my fault, of course. I apologize deeply. My dear girl, yes, I do apologize deeply."

It wasn't as in the dream, no velvet and pearls and fragrant embrace, but it was almost as good, the firm handshake and brushing kiss, the genuine look of appreciation in the dark, searching eyes.

"And William too, yes, how alike you are! As so you should be. Two for the price of one, how lucky for me!"

Mrs Scott was laughing. He embraced her and said, "What a happy day – I have you to thank, I know. I am so grateful to you, as always. What a rock you are in my dissolute life."

No laughter then, but a solemn acknowledgement, and Alice saw the motherly look on Mrs Scott's face directed with a secret sort of anguish at the man who looked, indeed, young enough to be her son.

Luckily Ellen and the others were at dancing school, and Mr Scott was out on the gallops, so it was just the four of them that went into the house together to take coffee in the sitting room. The doors were open into the garden and the birds were singing. Alice's heart was singing in accord. He was wonderful!

"Do you ride?" he asked Alice.

"Oh yes."

"That was how she came back into our lives," said Mrs Scott, and explained the embarrassing story.

"Perhaps we can ride out together this afternoon and get to know each other. Riding over the heath is my great love, and William, I am afraid, has no fondness for it. Eh, William? A look of great distress comes over him when I suggest it. Isn't that right?"

William smiled and said, "Yes. But I do when asked."

"And Mr Scott tells me I've got to make a decision about Snatchcorn. I've heard some very strange stories about you and Snatchcorn, Alice. I shall need to know more."

"Oh yes! I—"

95

"Later, Alice, when you go off together," Mrs Scott said. "We have a lot to talk about just now."

"Yes, Alice, give me an hour. Then we'll be off. Go and ask Mr Anderson to choose us two nice horses for our ride."

Alice went out with William, amazed. Mr Ticino had been her role model for a father, and she had never suspected they came like Lord Falkenburg. What a story for Mabel and Mrs Pinney! She longed to run home at once and spill it all out. But she had to do her father's bidding. She was nervous of Mr Anderson.

"What does he mean, choose two nice horses? Racehorses?"

"Yes, he always rides his own out. Don't worry. Anderson'll choose you an old sheep. He won't risk you on a bolter, not first time out. Or you can take Ellen's pony."

"No fear! She'd kill me."

William laughed. "Tell him you want one of your own. Keep him up to scratch!"

A pony of her own . . . what bliss! Was it possible? The others all had one, even William, and the grooms looked after them. But if she had one she would look after it herself.

She was nervous of Mr Anderson, asking him for two racehorses, but he seemed to understand the situation.

"There's none of the racehorses will stand for a side saddle, that's for sure. You'll have to ride one of the carriage horses – old Marshall will suit you. Unless you take Miss Ellen's—"

"No. Not Miss Ellen's." Alice was firm.

Marshall and Captain were the two chestnut carriage horses

that Mrs Scott drove out, much smarter than Daisy. They did everything, even a day's hunting if needed. Marshall was saddled, and a lad prepared a famous Gold Cup winner for his Lordship.

"His favourite – and so he should be, the money he's won."

They called him Henry but that was a nickname. He was a shining, arrogant bay, impeccably turned out. *How wonderful to ride such a horse!* Alice thought. She knew now what Robin was after, to work amongst these wonderful animals. She went indoors and changed into her habit, and then Lord Falkenburg came out and looked at his horses with Mr Anderson – he owned ten. He kept Alice by his side and told her all the races they had won. Then he legged her up on Marshall, who stood waiting with a lad at his head, and Mr Anderson legged him up on Henry and they rode out of the yard side by side.

It was the proudest moment of Alice's life. She felt she would burst inside her tightly buttoned habit, high on the smart chestnut with this handsome man – her father! – at her side.

"Ah, this is the life, Alice," he said, as the great sea of grass opened out ahead of them. "You can keep London and all that claptrap. I want to settle here and have my own stud and live like a country gent. Racing and hunting and training gun dogs. No more embassies and balls and nights in Monte Carlo. That's all for a young man. I want to be a family man now, with my twins near me."

"And Snatchcorn," suggested Alice.

"Ah, yes, and Snatchcorn. We have to decide about Snatchcorn, I am told."

"Yes. Did you know he was kept on a chain and never goes out?"

"I will see to it, Alice, I promise." He sounded suitably contrite. "I'll start riding him out."

"Ride him?" This startled Alice.

"Yes, I used to ride him, when he was in training. He is magnificent to ride."

Alice had a vision of herself, astride like a lad, galloping towards the horizon on her beloved Snatchcorn. One day, when he was tamed . . . yes, why not? Up here, on Marshall, her dreams knew no bounds.

And then they were cantering side by side, first slowly, then with lengthening strides up the short soft turf, both of them laughing, the man on the Gold Cup winner and the girl on the carriage horse. The accord was tangible. Of all the ways to be introduced to her father, this was the best, Alice knew. Her heart soared.

But at lunchtime, when the family was all together and Lord Falkenburg spoke of his pleasure in finding out how well his daughter could handle a horse, Alice was aware of Ellen's eyes on her from across the table. Her animosity was frightening. Alice could see how jealous she was of William, for a start, the boy taking pride of place in spite of not really belonging. William was cordial and clever and was bound to be liked, but Ellen could not bear her place being usurped. Now, with Alice's arrival, she was being doubly usurped. Especially in the presence of his Lordship, to whom the Scott parents deferred very respectfully — no doubt because he was the main source of their income. Alice found the naked hate deeply disturbing. It was all very well being told airily by William to take no notice, and being reassured by Mrs Scott that the girl would grow out of it, but Alice did not know how to handle the situation. It was true that everyone else seemed not to notice, but Alice knew it was no figment of her imagination. Ellen sat opposite her and Alice could not avoid the shafts of jealousy that seemed to her to cross the table like sword thrusts.

Mr Scott was telling his Lordship the story of Alice's empathy with Snatchcorn. Alice wished he wouldn't, not in front of Ellen, as of course she came in for more praise and approbation.

"But I'm afraid the horse must leave this yard, sir — I haven't a lad now, after two dispatched to hospital, who will go near the horse."

"Yes, we need to set up our own stud, where the mares can come and visit him. And he must have his own stallion man."

"Stallion woman. Alice," said William.

They all laughed. Alice thought, *Tom and Robin! Their own stud!*

"I must find a property," said Lord Falkenburg. "I need my own place and a home for the children, when they are ready to leave here."

"The old Lodge is empty and has several acres with it. It might suit," said Mr Scott.

They started talking about property and Alice sat with her mind reeling – their own place! A stud! And Snatchcorn to hand! And William! It was all too much to take in and she couldn't eat her treacle sponge. William ate it for her. She still felt like a visitor, yet her whole life was being remapped over the lunch table.

When they had finished her father said, "Let's go and visit this man-eater, Alice, and we'll decide what's to be done with him."

Mr Scott came with them. Snatchcorn's box was clean and he had hay in his manger, but he was still chained to the wall and could not attack them. Alice saw her father's face turn grim.

"This will never do! No horse can be kept like this and stay sane."

"I agree, sir, but there is no other way, if we keep him here."

"Take the chain off, at least. I will see to him. Alice and I will take charge."

"I'll take the chain off," Alice volunteered.

"Yes, let's see this magic," said her father.

They went into the box together, Alice talking to the troubled stallion all the time. She did not go close until he stopped champing and pulling at his chain. As usual her presence calmed him, and she was able to stand stroking his neck and then fondling his ears. She took the chain off and held him by his head collar. He nuzzled her shoulder and stood quietly.

"No one else can do that with him," Mr Scott said.

When Lord Falkenburg approached, Snatchcorn went for him. Alice pulled him back with all her strength, which wasn't sufficient. Snatchcorn got a mouthful of expensive tweed.

"It's her confidence, and being female, I think," said his Lordship, unperturbed. "It's only men that have tried to dominate him, no women. And she has no fear. It's wonderful."

"But he must go," said Mr Scott.

"Yes. I understand. Why don't we go and look at the old Lodge? Call on Ticino and see if he knows of a suitable place? I think putting the horse out to grass would settle him for the time being, with some old mare for company. He needs sweetening. We need a nice secure field. Shall we go together?"

"Yes, certainly."

"Put the stallion back, Alice. But no chain. No chain, ever again."

Alice did as she was told, and shot the bolts to on Snatchcorn's door. She laid her head on his silky neck as he came to look out, thrilled at the plan for his future. Her father was magic! He understood. She was flushed with pleasure and excitement.

"Well done," he said to her.

As the two men walked away down the drive Alice saw Mrs Scott and Ellen watching from the front door. Alice, on her own now, felt compelled to join them.

"That man!" said Mrs Scott, shaking her head. "He always shakes us all up when he comes. He's a real breath of fresh air."

"I think he's absolutely stupid," said Ellen, "unchaining that horse. It should be shot."

"Well, certainly, it will be better for us all if he takes him away." Mrs Scott sent Ellen an angry, warning look.

Alice glared at Ellen. "He's not stupid!"

"He is stupid. Bringing William here, and now you, lodging you here like a pair of racehorses whether we want you or not—"

"Ellen!" Mrs Scott suddenly turned bright red.

"He pays us to have you!" Ellen shouted at Alice. "We don't want you! You don't belong here—"

"Ellen, that's enough! THAT IS ENOUGH!"

Alice saw with a shock that Mrs Scott had lost her temper. Her face had gone even brighter red and she raised her hand as if she would strike her daughter. Ellen flinched back but her eyes sparked with malicious glee.

Mrs Scott hissed at her, "Apologize to Alice! Apologize at once! We invited them here! It is our pleasure and nothing to do with belonging."

"I won't apologize! He pays you! He pays you to look after his illegitimate children—"

"Ellen! How dare you!"

This time Mrs Scott lashed out to smack Ellen's face, but Ellen ducked and ran back into the house. Alice saw that she was laughing at having successfully delivered her accusation and poor Mrs Scott was traumatized at having lost control. Her ample bosom heaved dangerously above the tight corsets.

"Oh Alice, I'm so sorry!" She was almost weeping. "I seem to have no influence over her – she is so jealous! I don't know – she doesn't mean to be so hurtful."

She obviously did mean, Alice thought, astonished at the outburst. That word that William had warned her about – illegitimate – thrown like a brand. Was it so awful, to be illegitimate, born out of wedlock? She must ask Mabel as soon as possible. She needed to know these things! Mrs Scott put her arm round her, calming down with an obvious effort.

"You are a strong girl, Alice. I'm sure you will cope. You have a wonderful father and if he stays – as he is promising – you won't suffer."

Alice had no intention of suffering. It was not surprising that Ellen was jealous, after all, Lord Falkenburg being so obviously gorgeous as a father compared with the bad-tempered Mr Scott, and William for a twin was a real bonus. She was incredibly lucky, illegitimate or not. But living with Ellen was going to be a pain.

Everyone having disappeared, Alice decided to nip back home and tell Mrs Pinney and Mabel the goings-on, and report on her new father. They would be agog to hear the news.

It was a hot day and the dust flew up as she ran down the back road to the stable-yard. Ellen or no Ellen, her spirits were soaring. The stables were empty, but Robin was mucking out. His face lit up as Alice crashed through the gate.

"Alice!"

"Robin!"

They danced round each other, laughing.

"Cor, look at you! You do look posh!"

"I am posh! I am posh!"

"You're only silly old Alice!"

"And you're silly old Robin! I thought you were going to work in a racing yard?"

"I am! I start next week at old Robinson's. He thinks I'm going to be too heavy, but for the moment it's all right – he'll take me. That's great, isn't it?"

"You'll have to starve yourself, like a proper jockey."

"Yeah, and die! Mrs Pinney keeps giving me cake and biscuits."

"You have to say no."

"I can't! I can't!"

Alice was glad: she wanted him to come and work with Snatchcorn, along with his father.

"I've got to see Pinney. I'll send you out some biscuits."

She ran up the garden and burst into the kitchen.

Mrs Pinney and Mabel were sitting over cups of tea at the table. Their faces lit up and they jumped up to embrace her.

"Why, just look at you, in a new dress and all, and your hair. . .!"

They were all exclamations of delight and amazement, Mrs Pinney getting a fresh batch of biscuits out of a tin and Mabel finding some chocolates.

"How we do miss you!" they both said.

"And your father's arrived, Tom said, with his fine pair of horses which means he's staying over, so now you've met him at last. . ." Mrs Pinney's voice ended on an enquiring note, at which Alice poured out how lovely he was, how kind, how they had ridden on the heath, had lunch, seen Snatchcorn, planned a new life for him. . .

"And he's looking for a place of his own, for me and for William and Snatchcorn! The Lodge, he said—"

"What, that old place! It's been empty for years!"

"It's got a nice stable-yard, that's what will interest him," said Mabel.

"But the house! It's a ruin! If he had a wife, no wife would agree to it, that's for sure!"

"He hasn't got a wife," said Alice flatly.

The two women were silent suddenly and Alice burst out, "Why is it bad to be illegitimate? What does it mean? Ellen said—"

"Oh, that Ellen!" snorted Mrs Pinney. "She should know better than to bring up a thing like that. . ."

"But William said too – he said it was a scandal. We are a scandal! You must tell me! You know all these things."

"We don't know everything, my love," said Mrs Pinney sadly. "And we don't know who your dear mother is, for all the gossip that flies around. Only your father knows that, and it's him you should ask, if it's wise, which I doubt. If he wants you to know, he will tell you. But he's not married so yes, you are a scandal, my duck. Born out of wedlock. Illegitimate, as they say. Society doesn't hold with it, for all it's being going on since Adam and Eve and will continue to do so."

"It probably means you're a love child," said Mabel comfortingly.

"A love child?"

"They loved each other so much that they had you children, in spite of not being married."

"But if they loved each other so much why didn't they marry?"

"Because she is married to someone else, that is the only answer. And so she couldn't keep you, although I'm sure she wanted to."

Alice digested this. "But it's not our fault," she said, "not me and William's, so why is Ellen so horrid to us?"

"Ah, there's the rub. Of course it's not your fault, but people can be very cruel, as you've found out. It's something you've got to live with, Alice, as best you can. This is what Mr Ticino tried to shield you from, why he didn't send you to school."

Mabel said, "And of course Ellen is a horrid little snob, and just think how she feels, you having that lovely man for a father! And a lordship too. Even if it is a scandal, it makes you much better than her, doesn't it?"

"Even if I'm illegitimate?"

"There's no better about it," said Mrs Pinney with another of her snorts. "We're all God's children, equal in His eyes."

"And we're all snobs too," added Mabel.

"And that's an end to it," said Mrs Pinney. "You just hold your head up, Alice, and don't let these cruel people get you down. You are a very lucky girl, illegitimate or not."

"Yes, I think so."

"So, what's the house like? Have you got a nice bedroom to yourself? And is the cooking good? And that manservant, Charles, is he as pompous as he looks. . .?"

She had to answer all these questions and more besides, and she remembered to ask Mabel again if she would like a job there. She knew now that she herself would very much like Mabel to be there, in one of the servants' rooms on the top floor.

Mabel gave the same answer. "I'll come if you want me, if Mrs Scott wants me, if Mr Ticino will let me go. If Mrs Pinney doesn't mind."

"There's no future here for you," Mrs Pinney said. "But I'll miss you, daft girl that you are. I've brought you up to be real useful."

"Yes, you have, Mrs Pinney."

Alice was pleased with her visit and skipped back to her other home, sorry to have missed Robin. She was planning to get Robin a new job too. And Tom as well.

Poor Mr Ticino!

Chapter Seven

Alice slept heavily. At first her brain was whirling too much with all the excitements of her new life and she kept turning over and over with the visions that were bounding about into her head. But then, the great happiness cloaking her wits, she slept.

She awoke very suddenly, not knowing why. It was dark and still. There was a moon and she could see the shapes in her room and a brightness in the window, but nothing stirred. She thought at first it was the hard lump of Goldie down the bed that had woken her, but then she realized it was sound that had disturbed her sleep. What sound? She lay for a while, listening. She felt there was something wrong. But why? An owl hooted from the trees beyond the stables. There was a night man in the main racing-yard who was supposed to stay awake, with his dog, but all was quiet out there. The big gates were closed and locked. Even from her high window she could not see in. She knew race horses got nobbled, drugged, by villains, and all trainers had to keep a watch, but Mr Scott never seemed much worried.

But the feeling of unease made her get out of bed and go to her window to look out.

Snatchcorn's door was wide open! Not just his top door but his bottom door too, pulled back. His stable was empty. In the shadows she saw a white figure running from the stable-yard round the back corner of the house, returning. A white nightdress, a slight figure, long fair hair . . . just a glimpse. It was Ellen.

Alice was shocked rigid. Ellen had let Snatchcorn out. How could she do such a thing? How could she be so spiteful? It was against her, Alice, and against her father, to hurt them as much as possible. She spun round, opening her mouth to scream for help. Then stopped suddenly, appalled by the thought of the whole household knowing. Damning Ellen in front of them all; whatever good would come of it? Horrors would result.

She pulled on her old cardigan over her nightdress and crept out onto her landing. She heard Ellen come tiptoeing back up the stairs below and into her bedroom. Ellen's room was at the far end of the corridor from the guest room where Lord Falkenburg was sleeping, luckily. Alice closed her door and crept down her stairs. Her stairs came out right opposite the guest room door, thank goodness. Alice opened the door, her heart beating nervously.

Her father was fast asleep. He seemed to have no nightshirt on, and was sprawled face down, looking very peaceful.

Alice, even in this contingency, didn't know how to wake him, what to call him. Ralph?

She put a hand on the warm shoulder and shook it.

"Papa!" she said, for the first time in her life. It sounded wonderful, even under the circumstances. She said it again.

He stirred and slowly awoke. Seeing her anxious face was obviously something of a shock. She sensed the alarm.

"Snatchcorn's got out," she whispered. "His stable is empty."

At this he sat up immediately, wide awake.

"Whatever . . . how do you know? Did you see him go?"

"No. I just looked out, and the door is open."

Even to him, just at the moment, she did not want to say about Ellen. "Can we go and catch him, just ourselves, without waking everyone up?"

Her father swung his legs out of bed, clutching a sheet round his hips, and sat there for a moment, considering. Then he grinned widely and said, "Why not? What larks, Alice, you and me chasing a savage stallion all around the town in the dead of night! We don't want to wake the family, of course not! What a good idea! Run and get some clothes on."

Alice fetched another cardigan and pulled it on over her nightdress while her father got dressed, and in a moment they were creeping down the stairs like burglars. In spite of her anxiety, Alice was bubbling with excitement at conspiring in this adventure with her father. What a very unboring man he was! Not a bit like Mr Ticino or Mr Scott.

Once out in the home stable-yard he was brisk and purposeful.

"We want a bridle, and some titbits to tempt him."

Alice showed him where, and he put a few handfuls of oats into a bucket.

"The only way out is down the drive, so he must have gone that way. Then, unless he's grazing on the lawn, he'll have made for the gallops, the way he knows."

They hurried down the drive. Snatchcorn wasn't on the lawn or anywhere in the garden. Out on the road he could have gone either way.

"Maybe we should take a couple of horses. It might be a long way." Ralph hesitated.

Now she had called him Papa, Alice couldn't think of him as a lordship any more. He must be Ralph, now she knew him (although not to his face, of course).

She had a sudden, blinding idea.

"Daisy! We can take Daisy. She's just down the road."

She explained who Daisy was and he said a mare would be a good lure, and what a good idea, and they hurried along the lane and into her old stable-yard. Of course, Tom heard them and came down to see what was going on, but when he heard their quest he thought it a good idea to take Daisy.

"She's only got Miss Alice's side saddle, though," he said.

"Don't bother with a saddle. Just a bridle. We'll lead her out on the gallops and he might just come to her if we're lucky."

"Very well, sir."

It struck Alice as really funny to be standing in her old yard in her nightdress in the middle of the night, chatting with her father and Tom. It was warm and still and, apart from their hushed voices, quite silent. Just a faraway sad whinny, a mare having lost her foal perhaps, and a farm dog barking. A faint rustle in the grass, the sigh of a falling leaf . . . how strange, Alice thought, savouring the moment. She trusted completely in her father finding Snatchcorn.

Tom offered to help, but Ralph said, "No, go back to bed. This is our adventure, the two of us. I'm sure we'll catch him. And we'll bring Daisy back when we're done."

"Well, good luck, sir." And Tom gave Alice a smile and a wink, rejoicing in her turn of fortune, to have found such a splendid father.

They went along the lane and out onto the gallops, leading Daisy. There was no sign of Snatchcorn. They stood on the edge of the town looking up at the sea of grass that stretched before them in the moonlight, but nothing moved.

"He must be here," Ralph said. "He wouldn't have crossed town."

"But he might be a long way away."

"True."

They took the way Snatchcorn was used to, and after a bit Ralph decided they might as well ride. He took a flying vault onto Daisy's back, and hauled Alice up after him. She sat behind him, astride, in spite of her nightdress. She had always longed to ride astride like a boy, and now she was, her bare legs feeling the soft warmth of Daisy's flanks, her arms round her father's waist.

"You all right?" he called over his shoulder.

"Oh yes!" More all right than she could ever remember being in her life.

He walked at first, and they looked and looked, but saw nothing in the darkness. The horse was the colour of the dark, after all. But then they grew bored and Ralph said, "How about a canter to the top? Can you cope?"

"Yes!"

Daisy had an easy lollopy canter and Alice found no trouble in staying in place, holding on to her father. He sat so easily bareback, part of the horse, and Daisy recognized his skill and went like a thoroughbred, no doubt enjoying the soft turf and the starlight like themselves. But at the top they scoured the woods without success.

Ralph pulled up.

"Dammit," he said. "We don't want him out here when day comes and all the rogues in Newmarket will be after him. He might even get shot if he's recognized. But I suppose it's a bit daft trying to see him in the dark. If he were grey, perhaps. . ."

They stood still, the only sound the puffing of old Daisy's breath. But then the mare suddenly raised her head and whinnied.

Her two riders froze.

"There!" whispered Alice.

Something moved in the trees. There was a rustle and snapping of twigs and a darker form moved against the dark background. A snort and the ripple of a deep-throated whicker. The horse moved out into the open and stood looking at them.

"Snatchcorn," whispered Alice.

"Slip off," her father ordered.

They moved in accord, very quietly and tactfully. Ralph passed Alice the bucket with the oats rustling in the bottom and murmured, "Just go up to him, quietly."

She approached him, talking her usual endearing rubbish, which he recognized. Her voice was soft and kindly. He let out his low whicker of welcome and she gave him the oats, and her father came up and slipped the bridle into her hand as the horse ate. Snatchcorn snapped at him and put back his ears, but no more.

"See if you can get him to take it."

Snatchcorn made no demur. Alice did up the throat lash and handed the reins to her father.

Snatchcorn was safe.

"Oh, wonderful, wonderful!" murmured Ralph. "You are a magician, Alice. I don't think he would have come to anyone else. He'd have led them on a wild chase all over Suffolk and got himself injured."

The oats gone, Snatchcorn turned his attention to Daisy, who put back her ears and started kicking. It had proved right that the stallion had been attracted by the mare, but now it seemed to be causing a fracas. To Alice's astonishment Ralph quickly took Snatchcorn's bridle, and with one of his athletic vaults was on his back, turning him away. Even without a saddle he had perfect control.

"He can't bite me up here," he shouted.

Alice laughed. It was the last thing she had imagined.

"You can ride Daisy, can't you?" he called.

"Yes, if I can get on."

She led Daisy along by the trees until she found a fallen log that gave her the required height. Daisy stood helpfully as Alice hitched up her nightdress and scrambled aboard. How strange it felt, astride and bareback! Without her father she felt rather unsafe. The side saddle gripped a body in such a way that it was quite difficult to fall off but this seat was slippery, with no grip at all except from her own knees.

"Sit up, relax," her father said, coming alongside. "We'll just go slowly, while you get used to it."

Alice could see that Snatchcorn was dying to take off, but her father was such a good rider that he was able to calm the horse without seeming to do anything, just sitting quietly, his hands soft on the reins. Daisy's company calmed the stallion too. He wasn't used to being out alone and had no doubt been quite alarmed by his freedom. Gradually he quietened, and as they walked back towards the sleeping town below, the first light of dawn crept into the sky behind them. The moon paled and an early morning mist lay around them like cobwebs. The air was sharp, full of the dawn chorus of skylarks. Alice felt she was bursting with happiness. It was so strange and beautiful out here with her father for company, and he so graceful and kind on her beloved Snatchcorn. *Thank you, Ellen*, she thought, *for giving me this wonderful night*.

But as they came nearer home and the novelty of it all had slightly worn off, she thought she ought to tell Ralph truly what had happened. It wasn't only herself that Ellen had tried to hurt, but him too.

She said, "Snatchcorn didn't get out by himself. Ellen let him out. I saw her."

"Ellen? Whatever for?"

"To get at me. She hates me."

"Oh dear." Ralph was quiet for a bit. Then he said, "That's difficult."

"I don't think we should say, though. Just pretend I happened to look out and see the door open."

"But. . ." He was unconvinced. Then, "Maybe. You know best. But perhaps a quiet word with Mrs Scott? She might do something worse if she thinks she's failed in this."

"A secret, though. No one else."

"No. No one else. And perhaps not even Mrs Scott. I'll think about it."

They rode on quietly, and saw lights coming on, blinking, in the grey town they were approaching. Alice felt cold now, and suddenly very sleepy.

"How lucky you saw," Ralph said. "And that we caught him. He will be a star as a sire, Alice, I know he will. We must find the right home for him, his own yard, and paddocks. And a place there for us too."

"Oh yes!"

They went down past the big stables and into the lane that led to Daisy's stable. Tom was up to meet them, and all eyes to see his Lordship riding Snatchcorn.

"My word, you were lucky, sir! I thought he could be out all week."

"Yes, me too! What a catastrophe averted! And all thanks to Alice."

"Yes, she's a bright button, our Alice."

He took Daisy as Alice slid off.

Ralph then rode Snatchcorn up to the mounting block and said to Alice, "Get up here with me, Alice. You can ride him home."

Alice could not believe her ears. Tom looked alarmed.

"Why, sir, is he safe enough for the girl?"

"Yes. He was never a difficult ride. I used to ride him out on exercise with the string when he was racing. It's different in the stable, I admit. He eats lads for breakfast, he senses their fear. I doubt if we can cure that in a hurry, but I swear to you he won't harm Alice between here and his stable."

"I'll take your word for it, sir."

And Alice climbed the mounting block and he bunked her the last bit to get her leg over Snatchcorn's withers, in front of her father this time. How high she felt! The lean dark neck ahead of her seemed to stretch for miles, and her legs were no longer stretched over a broad back, merely hanging comfortably down on either side of the great bones of the horse's shoulders. The withers hummocked in front of her crotch, holding her in place, and her father's arms encircled her to hold the reins.

Whatever was to happen in all the rest of her life, Alice thought she would never forget the happiness of the few minutes it took to ride back to the racing stable in the embrace of her father and her dear Snatchcorn.

Chapter Eight

It was just as well she remembered her magic adventure with her father so vividly, for it was to sustain her in the difficult days that followed. Ellen took every opportunity to make her life a misery, mostly out of Mrs Scott's presence, and Alice was only kept sane by William's staunch support and the eager love of what they called the little girls. The little girls had no great love for Ellen either, with her bossy ways and sulks, and informed on Ellen to their mother, although Alice never did. The situation was a great worry for Mrs Scott, who was endlessly patient with poor Ellen, convinced she would soon "grow out of it".

But William said, "People don't grow out of their nature."

Nothing Ellen said or did to William ever ruffled him, so she took to the new threat of Alice with relish. Alice hadn't William's stoicism and found it hard to ignore the spite. She went back home and poured out her aggravations to Mrs Pinney and Mabel. They were full of indignation and Mabel determined to take up Alice's suggestion that she get the job of housemaid with Mrs Scott.

"I'll look after you, my pet, and show that Miss Ellen where she gets off."

"Get yourself the sack in the first week," said Mrs Pinney sniffily. "You mark my words, it'll be no holiday at that place, all them rooms to service."

"No, well, better than being bored in a place like this."

"You're right, I suppose."

"That adventure of yours with the horse must've made her real mad," said Mabel.

"Yes. She saw us come back. I saw her face at the window. And Papa never said a word to anyone, not even that Snatchcorn had got out. We got back just before the lads came in."

"My word, how it must've riled her!"

Mrs Scott took Mabel on, and gave her a room on the same floor as Alice, saying quite severely, "You must remember she is a servant, Alice. You're not to be too familiar with her. It's unseemly."

Certainly Mabel's room was very servantish compared with Alice's, almost a cupboard, with her bed squashed under the eaves so that if she sat up she banged her head. She had a small chest and a smaller washstand. She had to get up at five o'clock to do the downstairs rooms before the family got up, and set the breakfast table. There were no fires because it was summer, but Alice could see what labour that was going to be when winter came, all the fireplaces in every room to be cleaned out, relaid and lit, and the coal scuttles filled before breakfast. She also had to bring up hot water in cans to every bedroom, including Alice's.

"I'll fetch my own," said Alice staunchly.

"You will not!" said Mabel firmly.

She cleaned all day, helped in the kitchen, laid and served lunch, ironed all afternoon, did tea, and helped prepare dinner, waited on, cleared away, and made the bedrooms ready for night. She was finished at nine. Alice lamented at the amount of work, but Mabel laughed and said it was the same at home on the farm. "But them's animals. Humans are worse! More pernickety."

Apparently, as servant jobs went it was quite a good one. "Mrs Scott's easy, and the rest of the staff are nice enough. That Charles, he's a right laugh downstairs."

Alice couldn't see the stiff manservant being much of a laugh, but took Mabel's word for it. She was too shy to venture downstairs.

Papa, meanwhile, was anxious to find his own place and was looking at possibilities with Mr Ticino. Whether his twins were going to live with him or stay at the Scotts' had not been quite decided. It depended on what sort of a place he found, whether it was suitable, and whether they wanted to move.

When Alice asked William whether he wanted to move, he said gloomily, "It doesn't matter much. I'm being packed off to boarding school in September."

"William! Do you want to go?"

"No."

"I don't want you to go!"

"No. I wouldn't mind except for. . ." He broke off, doubtful.

"Except for what?"

"Well, you know. Our mother and all that. I shall get terrible ribbing, being illegitimate."

"Why should they know?"

"Oh, Alice, in those circles – they all know! Some of them might even know who our mother is! Some of 'em won't talk to me, I bet, and those that do will make my life a misery. I can see it all coming."

Alice knew about snobbery as it was all around them. Servants were inferior people. Who your parents were and what they did mattered terribly. It had never affected her much in the past, her best friends being the servants, but then she had never moved in the circles where these things mattered. It had mattered to Mr Ticino obviously, else he would never have kept her under wraps for so long. He was the sort of man who would never want to challenge convention, she knew now. He must have found his situation very difficult, but being paid for it must have helped. He liked money. Now at Mrs Scott's it seemed that her illegitimacy made it impossible for her to be integrated into the circle of her children's friends. Mrs Scott would not let her be included in the girls' outings with other mothers and children as she wasn't "acceptable". Mrs Scott did not mention this to Alice in so many words, but Alice noticed how often she was excluded with very poor excuses: "You can't go with a cold, Alice, spreading germs," and, "There are too many of you – Mrs Pointer's constitution is very frail. I think it would be best if you stayed behind, Alice."

William pointed out to her the real reason for these exclusions. "They never take me, but then I never want to go. So that's all right." But he could see that Alice wanted to go. She wanted to move in a wider circle and meet other girls. She longed for bosom girlfriends like she read about in books, the laughing girls she saw in the schoolyard and at church. At church a lot of women cut her dead, when they would speak with Mrs Scott and Ellen. Ralph never came.

He said to her, "It's time we moved on. I have found a place which suits perfectly for founding our stud, but the house is terrible. It will take time and money to make it nice. I'll take you to see it, and you can tell me what you think."

He spoke to her as if she were adult. He told William as well, but told Alice, "I don't think William is much interested in where he lives. He lives in his own world, with his books and his science. He is very independent."

Yes, Alice supposed that was true. William never seemed ruffled by what went on around him. He spent a lot of time alone in his room with microscopes and things. He didn't seem to need other people much, save his tutor, to whom he was very attached: a pale young man who came from Cambridge and had very little conversation with anyone else. The tutor had told Ralph that William needed to go to public school.

Alice could tell that the idea worried Papa, presumably for the reason that William had already told her about.

123

"Public school life is very cruel, when you are a newcomer," he said to Alice.

"Only if you are illegitimate," said Alice.

"Cruel to every newcomer, but worse, yes, if you are illegitimate."

"Was it cruel to you?"

Alice knew that Papa had proper parents, now deceased.

"Oh yes, horrible."

"How horrible?"

"Oh, they hide your books, they take your clothes, they put a dead rat in your bed, they hold your head under the cold tap till you nearly drown, they hold you out of the upstairs window by your ankles, they pretend they're stone deaf, they—"

"Oh, don't! For ever?"

"No, just when you're new. And only afterwards if you show that it makes you cry. It's called bullying. Once you show it doesn't affect you, they will get tired of it and leave you alone and then after that school's quite fun."

Alice could see why William was not too keen on going to school. Did he know all this? He seemed to have some idea. Alice decided not to think about it, it was so horrible.

Papa took her to see the place he had found. It was on the other side of town down a leafy drive between two smart new mansions with big stable-yards. The drive was overgrown and potholed, the prospect uninviting.

"These new houses were built in the grounds of this old run-down place. They were going to knock the old place down, but when I said I might make an offer for it they held fire. Now, what do you think?"

Whoever had lived in this place, must have died long ago, Alice thought. It was totally overgrown, the house standing amongst a wilderness of sycamore saplings and wild roses. The drive led in a sweep to the front door, which no longer existed. In front had once been lawn, but it was now full of high weeds and thistles. The house was very ugly, its stucco grey and cracked, its long sash windows gaping. It was not very big, although it had grand steps up to an extravagant portico. Ivy covered many blemishes. A family of young crows sat cawing on the cracked chimneys.

"Oh, I like it," said Alice, fancying having it all to herself. It was a private little world of its own, tucked neatly away out of sight in a sort of forest, and yet only about five minutes from the high street. It just needed a few repairs and some paint. Compared with the elegant new mansions in what had once been its park, it looked very humble.

"It could be all right," said Papa, obviously pleased with her remark. "I can't imagine what Mrs Scott would think of it, but then. . ." He shrugged, then smiled.

"She needn't see it," said Alice.

The drive went past the house and continued into a stable-yard, which was in far better repair than the house, and looked only recently emptied. It had about twelve boxes facing each other, and a carriage house and feed barn facing. Between these two sheds was an archway and gate that led directly into fenced paddocks surrounded by trees. Alice could see at once that it was the stable-yard and paddocks that were the attraction. They were indeed perfect for housing Snatchcorn and his mares.

"And room to expand, if we need it," Ralph said eagerly. "And there's a nice groom's place over the carriage house, so no problem about having a man on hand."

"Maybe Tom would come, Mr Ticino's groom," said Alice quickly. "You met him – you know – he's so nice—"

"We can't take all Mr Ticino's staff! We've already taken Mabel—"

"And Daisy, for Snatchcorn's companion!" Alice cried. "The very thing! Mr Ticino was always saying he needs a new horse, she's too old. He's going to send her to the knackers – will you buy her?"

"Perhaps if I buy him a new horse he will let us have her. It would be a good thing to give Snatchcorn a companion if we turn him out. It might be just the thing to settle him."

They made plans like two conspirators. Ralph liked all Alice's ideas, and Alice loved having her father all to herself. But was he always going to live here in Newmarket with her, the two of them together in this house?

When she asked him this question, his enthusiasm suddenly died. They happened to be sitting on the front steps of the old house in the warmth of the autumn sun. Ralph was wearing his old tweed jacket and breeches and a tweed cap pushed back on his head, and looked to Alice very like William at that moment – William thinking about going to boarding school.

He said, "I am coming to live in Newmarket, yes. But just now, until Christmas, I have to be in London quite a lot. You will have to stay at the Scotts' until then. And you will have a hard time, Alice, if you go to school. I'm warning you. Because you have no mother and your father is unmarried and a great source of local gossip. If you want you can have a private governess, and have lessons at home."

"No. I don't want to share lessons with Ellen. I want to go to school."

"You're sure about this?"

"Yes, very sure."

"I just wish it could be easier for you. I've put a great burden on you two children, I'm afraid."

"I don't mind! Really I don't!"

"Well, you're a tough potato. You'll rise above 'em, I daresay. But I wish I could be here to see you through it. My mission in London is to do with your mother, Alice – I tell you this in confidence. Maybe, just maybe, the outcome will be successful, and we shall all be together at last, but life isn't always how we want it to be, I don't have to tell you that."

Alice sat on the step, her heart pounding at having at last received an intimation that her mother existed, was still there for her. In London? Her real mother! The eternal question trembled on her lips: "Who is our mother?"

It took all her courage to ask it.

"I can't tell you, Alice."

"Why not?"

"It is too much to put on you, this confidence. Just now, that is. Unfair, I know. I can't tell you how sorry I am, to have made your life so difficult."

The never-ending mystery! *Why, why, why?*

She tried to make her voice steady and calm. "My life isn't difficult," she lied. "My life is wonderful. Don't be sorry!"

"I will get this house put right, and after Christmas we will live here together and run our stud. Whatever the outcome, that is for certain."

With that Alice had to be content. The conversation had amazed her, that she had been taken so far into her father's confidence. He put his arm round her and gave her a hug, and then they went through the house and decided what the builders would have to do, and Ralph agreed to go and see Mr Ticino and buy Daisy off him, and buy him a new horse and gig to make him happy. And poach Tom.

"Tom could still work for Mr Ticino. If Snatchcorn is turned out, he won't be much work."

"The house over the stable here is much better than at Mr Ticino's. I'm sure Tom will be glad to move," said Alice. *And Robin too*, she thought.

"Yes, and the sooner we move Snatchcorn the better. You will do that, Alice – your privilege to lead him to his new home."

"You could ride him!"

"No. I want you to do it."

"But it's right through town."

"Yes. I want everyone to see. It's called advertising. It shows our man-eater is a tame kitten at heart."

Alice felt faint.

Chapter Nine

First Alice and Robin took Daisy to her new home. Mr Ticino had agreed eagerly to receiving a smart new horse and new gig in exchange. When Alice went to him with Ralph to discuss it, he actually gave her a peckish kiss and laughed, saying how well she looked. Alice nearly died of shock. Later she decided he must be much happier no longer having the worry of her, and all those secrets to keep. How amazing!

Alice insisted on calling her new home Paradise.

"Paradise!" snorted Robin. "Some paradise!"

They turned Daisy out in the field and she fell to grazing without any fuss.

"Good. Now we'll fetch Snatchcorn," Ralph said.

Alice's job, her hour of glory. Mr Scott, Mr Anderson and all the stable lads to come out to watch, goggle-eyed with fright. All the other lads in Newmarket too were agog to know how it would go, and lurked in groups across the Severalls to watch. Mrs Scott came out into the yard with the rest of the family, including William, but kept well out of the way. Tom and Robin came over to help.

"My word, but he's a beauty!" Tom said, as Alice went into the loose box.

"And he's ours!" Alice whispered.

"In a manner of speaking, perhaps."

Snatchcorn lunged over his door at Tom and Tom took a smart step backwards. Alice moved forward and said, "Don't be naughty now! You've got to be nice to Tom, like you are to me."

She stood and talked to him until his ears came forward, and Ralph handed her a bridle. He brought her a box to stand on, so she could reach. It was harder to put on than the head collar, but Alice was well-taught by Tom and managed it without too much trouble. She had managed it before up in the dark on Newmarket Heath when it was much harder. Snatchcorn's ears remained forward.

A long lead rein was attached to the bridle. Alice held it up close and led the stallion out into the yard. The onlookers all fell hastily back. Alice talked soothingly to Snatchcorn.

"You're a lucky boy – you're going to Paradise! The one here, not in Heaven. You must behave, Snatchcorn. It's your only chance now, to stay alive."

If they shot him, she knew he wouldn't go to Heaven. She couldn't bear to think of Snatchcorn in the Other Place. She talked to him and stroked his nose. He dropped his head and nuzzled at her.

"Are you ready?" Mr Scott asked her.

"Yes, we can go now."

Mr Scott insisted that a few large lads with pitchforks made up the procession. He had a gun in his pocket. He had no faith in the stallion, having had so much trouble over the years.

Everybody melted away as Snatchcorn stepped out. Only Robin nipped in close. His eyes were shining.

"Cor, Alice, this is really something!"

Several gardeners lined the gravel drive, pretending to be weeding. Snatchcorn walked beside Alice like a lamb. A knot of people stood round the gate.

"Get out of the way!" shouted Mr Scott angrily.

They scattered.

Alice had eyes only for Snatchcorn. She talked to him all the time. People had come out to stare all along the way, at her as much as the horse. Having been seen out in public with her father, with everyone knowing that she was to be set up in the old ruin when it was restored, she was the present hot gossip. They all whispered and gossiped, nannies with prams, and quite smart ladies, and butcher's boys and people going shopping, as well as all the lads who could manage it. Mr Scott was hating it, and Mr Anderson swore under his breath.

"What a circus!" Mr Scott breathed. And then, angrily, "Clear off! Clear off!"

But it was a public road. Not much interesting happened in the week and this was interesting. Word had got around about Alice's magic. The horse was well-known, notorious, for the death and injuries he had caused. Yet he walked serenely, pointing his elegant hooves and bending his neck to touch the little girl at his head.

"What a picture!" the old ladies sighed. Old ladies in Newmarket knew enough about the trade to recognize an amazing sight when they saw it. The boys with the pitchforks dropped sheepishly back. Mr Anderson stopped sweating and Mr Scott began to smile.

Alice chatted away. She told Snatchcorn all about his new field and his kind companion Daisy and how happy he would be and how Robin and Tom would feed him, and groom him too if he would let them. Her soft cheerful voice flowed over the stallion, who only knew abrupt, angry resonances. No fear flowed from her presence, as it did from everyone else he knew. There was no vibration of tension, only the funny flow of a gentle voice and the loving presence. Snatchcorn had never come across such a thing before. Fiery as a colt, he had always been handled with violence, "to teach him who is master". But Snatchcorn's nature was not to bend, to give in, but always to fight. That had made him a brilliant racehorse, but not a horse beloved by his grooms. Subsequent attempts to teach him a lesson had resulted in his getting more and more dangerous.

Perhaps the spectators were disappointed. They drifted away and the small procession turned into the drive to Paradise unnoticed. The shade of late summer closed over the girl and the horse, dappling the already dappled coat of the acquiescent stallion. Snatchcorn took in the new scenes without excitement, looking about him yet not pulling on the rein, bending his neck kindly to Alice's hand.

"It's a blooming miracle, that kid," said Mr Anderson to his boss. "I've never seen anything like it in my life."

The two men stood back as Alice led Snatchcorn across the empty yard to the gate into the field. Ralph opened the gate into the paddock. Daisy, grazing at the bottom, lifted her head and looked up enquiringly.

Ralph whispered to Alice, "Keep your fingers crossed!"

"He won't hurt her!" Alice was suddenly frightened.

"No. He's never attacked horses, only humans."

But turning Snatchcorn out loose was a worrying moment. What if he took off and jumped the fence? Anything might happen. He hadn't been let loose since he was a yearling (except for his night-time escapade a couple of weeks ago).

Alice exchanged the bridle for a head collar, and let him go.

All he did was put his head down and start grazing ravenously, as if he hadn't been fed for days.

"Well," they all said. And, "Well, I never!'

They waited, but nothing exciting happened at all. Daisy came down the field and snorted at him, and he nibbled her tail a little and went back to grazing. Daisy stayed near him. Their two muzzles rippled through the grass side by side.

"She'll have a foal," Robin said to Alice.

"Why?" Alice asked.

Robin went red and did not reply.

Alice had never thought of it. Now she did, she could not imagine anything more delightful, her two darlings producing a third darling. How life was improving! Ralph put his hand on her shoulder approvingly.

"You're a winner, Alice. With you in charge, our stud will flourish."

Alice turned to Ralph suddenly and flung her arms round him. It rose up in her almost like she was going to be sick – she couldn't help the tide of emotion. Pure love and gratitude for what had happened to her after her scrubbed, cold life with Mr Ticino. It was frightening, the ferocity of it. Ralph, holding her, was moved, chastened by having neglected her, but he covered it with amusement, a slight embarrassment.

"There, Alice, you're fine. That was splendid."

He thought – they all thought – it was a nervous reaction from delivering Snatchcorn safely, but it wasn't. She had had no doubts about that.

Now that Snatchcorn was moved, Tom and Robin took residence in the stable-yard. They could both still work for Mr Ticino as well for the time being, and he liked the arrangement, not having to pay them so much money. Alice longed to join them but knew it was quite impossible. William departed for Rugby, white-faced, with his trunk of books and clothes, and Alice's name was enrolled in an expensive school for young ladies in the town. She had rather fancied being in the big classroom she had eavesdropped on during her walks with Mabel, but Mrs Scott said that was for the common children.

"Alice is common," said Ellen.

"I'm not. My father's a lord," said Alice.

"And your mother's a—"

"Ellen!" screamed Mrs Scott.

"A lady!" said Alice.

"She's a—"

Mrs Scott slapped Ellen hard round the face and Ellen shrieked and ran out of the room. Mrs Scott burst into tears. Alice stood gaping.

"It's all right," said Alice staunchly. "It's not your fault."

She thought it was, in a way, for having so awful a daughter as Ellen, but perhaps one couldn't help these things.

Later Ellen made it plain to Alice that she would have a terrible time at school.

"It's a wonder they will take you. I suppose he's bribed them."

"Yes, I expect so." It infuriated Ellen when Alice didn't rise to her bait.

Alice tried to show that she was perfectly confident about starting school, but after what Ralph had said she was in fact very nervous. She kept reminding herself that she was "a tough potato".

Ralph had departed behind his beautiful white horses two days before her first day. His parting words were firmly fixed in Alice's head: "Remember, they all know about your leading a wild man-eating horse alone through the town – none of them could have done it. You've a reputation in more ways than one."

She suspected that that was the reason he had not done the job himself. He was a clever man.

On her first morning of school she wore a dark dress (regulation) with a white pinafore over the top. Mrs Scott tied her hair back with navy-blue ribbons. She had sent the lingering Ellen sharply to her own schoolroom with Amelia, and attended to Alice with affectionate concern.

"You are such a smart girl, Alice. I'm sure you'll have no trouble."

"Has William had trouble?"

"Well, truth to tell, we've had no word from him, apart from the stipulation weekly letter saying he is well and sends his love. No news at all. It rather worries me. He's a very sensitive boy, after all. But brave. He'll survive, I daresay."

She did not sound convinced. She gave Alice a hug and said, "But there, you've got a kind home to run back to, so it's not the same. And I'll send you off with Mabel, even if you do know the way."

For a stand-in mother, Mrs Scott wasn't bad, Alice thought. It was a comfort having Mabel.

"Just let them say anything bad to you, and I'll tell them where they get off, my duck," Mabel said fiercely.

"Oh, but you can't come into school, Mabel. Only to the entrance."

"Do me good, to learn a thing or two," Mabel said. "Write, for one thing. D'you think they'd take me?"

They got the giggles then, walking out to the Bury Road. A few other girls in little groups, wearing the same dark dresses, were walking the same way. Although she laughed, Alice felt her skin growing tight and her stomach sick. She hurried on to keep ahead of them, and when they came to the door of the school, a large house on the edge of town with a garden all round it, she almost thrust Mabel away.

"I'm all right now. Goodbye!"

"Good luck, my pet."

The school was for young gentlewomen, but Alice knew that the girls would be mostly daughters of tradespeople and trainers and professional men. None of them would boast a lord for a father, as she did. She kept telling herself this, to make up for the terrible stain of her illegitimacy. Even if she had not been warned and had rushed in with her usual impetuosity, she would soon have realized something was up. It was almost as if the girls were afraid of her, as if she were Snatchcorn himself. They drew away, and no one had a greeting. Even the teacher, a young, corseted, flustered woman called Miss Pomfret, found it difficult to speak to her as if she were a human being. She seemed covered in embarrassment.

"You are . . . you are. . ." If she remembered the name, she could not bring herself to speak it.

"Alice Ticino."

"Ah yes. Alice Ticino. From Mrs Scott?"

"I live with Mrs Scott."

"I am expecting you. Ah, Mrs Anstey. . ." She turned as a very large elderly woman waddled into the room. She had a huge bosom and several chins, and beady, unkind eyes. "This is our new girl, Alice Ticino."

The eyes needled her, the downturned lips showing no smile of welcome.

"Yes," she said. "I took her on condition that she kept herself to herself. Don't put yourself forward, young woman, do you understand me?"

Alice didn't, but thought it best not to say so. Mrs Anstey's bosom was so large she couldn't help putting herself forward, she thought.

"Yes, ma'am," she said.

"She can sit on her own, Miss Pomfret. Remember, several mothers have said they will take their girls" – she said "gels" – "away if she makes approaches to them."

"Certainly, Mrs Anstey. I will see to it."

Alice was given a table and chair at the side of the classroom all by herself. All the other girls sat at long desks shared by four or six, clustered together. It was as if she had chicken pox or scarlet fever. None of them spoke to her or even looked at her, save a girl called Henrietta who sat at the back, on the same side of the room as Alice. She was a four-square girl dressed carelessly, with straight black hair cut in an unfashionable fringe which dangled over eyes as dark. Her boots were muddy. All the other girls were primped up like Ellen, with fashionable hair and frills, and they giggled together, sending her sideways glances. It was like Ellen's party. She could hear the softest hisses of her name repeated, *Alice Ticino*, and she could see their lips forming the inevitable "She's not really Mr Ticino's daughter."

How stupid of them to make the remark, she thought, now that Lord Falkenburg had publicly taken her out and been seen with her and paid off Mr Ticino with a smart new horse and gig. Surely that much gossip had reached them by now? She wanted to stand up squarely and say, "I am Lord Falkenburg's daughter, you stupid apes," but she kept herself silent, her eyes downcast, her bosom (such as it was) squashed in.

The lessons were for girls far more stupid or ill-educated than herself. She knew the answer to every question and shot her hand up the fastest each time, but Miss Pomfret never asked her for her answer. After a while she stopped bothering. It was not very nice being ignored. When it came to written work she finished it before everyone else, and sat with her arms folded, waiting. The other girls leaned inelegantly over their books, breathing heavily. Alice sat and admired her beautiful writing. Miss Pratt had taught her better than she knew. But she had always been a taskmaster; that's why Alice had hated her lessons so.

But when it came to mid-morning break, when they all ran out into the garden chattering and laughing, no one spoke to her or even looked at her. She followed them out and stood on the path, but it was as if she was a stone statue standing in the way. They all rounded her without a glance, or sent sideways stares and made whispered remarks to their companions. It was humiliating in the extreme and made Alice feel dreadful. But she held on to her father's remark: she was a tough potato. Stick it out. They surely could not keep this up for ever?

The girl with the black fringe was the only one who looked her in the eye, speculative, although she did not speak. She did not join the big chatterers either, but talked in a bored way with another quieter girl. Alice noticed she had some wisps of straw on the back of her skirt.

So the day progressed. It was really terrible to realize you didn't exist. Far worse than being taunted or kicked. By the end of the afternoon it was very hard to sit upright in her desk, bright-eyed, as if it didn't matter. But then she remembered she was her father's daughter. This was the cause of the trouble, of course, but her father was brave and expected her to be brave. None of the other girls could tame Snatchcorn. Snatchcorn! He would be her saviour. Think of Snatchcorn all the time: she would not give in.

In her written work she came out top every day. This did not help her cause. She skated with contempt over the easy work that began to bore her. She thought of Snatchcorn and her stud. She thought of him all the time to stop herself from giving way to despair. She told Mrs Scott she was having a lovely time, and only Mabel knew the truth. Mrs Scott could well have guessed the truth with her motherly eye, but said nothing.

Ellen asked questions to needle: "Who have you made

friends with? What are their names? Have you been asked to tea?" Her eyes gleamed with satisfaction. "Have you met Eleanor Stitch? Nellie Portman?" Did she know from these girls who were her friends that she, Alice, sat alone and unapproached?

But on the third day of the second week the girl with the black fringe, whose name was Henrietta, came in late. She had straw on her skirt and muddy boots again, Alice noticed. She came past Alice's desk and said quite clearly, "Good morning, Alice," before she said, "Good morning, Miss Pomfret. I'm sorry I'm late. My pony lost a shoe."

Everyone goggled at her but she was perfectly at ease and sat down in her place at the back of the class. Alice felt a great warm glow spread all over her. Miss Pomfret gave her an uncertain look. When the lessons commenced Alice had the heart to put her hand up again when questions were asked. At the very end of the last lesson Miss Pomfret looked to her and said, "Well, Alice, what is the highest mountain in the world?"

"Mount Everest in the Himalayas, twenty-nine thousand feet."

Everyone stared at her and giggled. They looked embarrassed. Miss Pomfret too went red and pressed on with giving out homework instructions, more flustered than usual. Alice registered that she had made a breakthrough and her heart soared. When they went outside at last Alice went up to Henrietta and said, "Thank you."

Henrietta smiled.

She said, "My father is friends with your father."

Alice panicked. Which one?

"Mr Ticino?" she ventured.

"No. Lord Falkenburg. He has a couple of horses with my father. He stopped Snatchcorn from being destroyed, didn't he? My father said that would have been a criminal act."

"Oh yes! Yes it would!"

Dear Snatchcorn had saved her life, as she had saved his! Let her father take the credit, but she knew that it was she who had saved him. And Henrietta's father, a big trainer eight kilometres out of town, had recognized their wisdom.

Henrietta rode in and out to school on a pony she stabled behind a public house nearby. The ride took her under half an hour, using the gallops out of town. Her pony, a small black gelding called Daybreak, was sired by a Derby winner out of her mother's shopping pony. "A mistake," Henrietta said, "but what a good one!"

"I haven't got a pony," Alice said wistfully. She couldn't ride Daisy any more, as Snatchcorn went potty if Daisy left his sight. Snatchcorn was in love with Daisy.

Henrietta was surprised at this remark and so was Alice when she thought about it.

"You could ride up and visit me if you had a pony," Henrietta said.

"I could probably borrow one of the carriage horses."

"Or Ellen's. She's got a nice pony she hardly ever rides."

"Oh, I couldn't borrow Ellen's! She'd kill me."

Henrietta laughed. "I'll get my father to tell Lord Falkenburg that you need a pony. Or you could tell him yourself."

"He's in London, until Christmas. I won't see him."

"Ah well, at Christmas then. I'll tell my father to tell him the next time he sees him. Or you could write to him, couldn't you? Ask him."

Henrietta didn't seem to mind about Alice's stigma, being much more concerned by her lack of such an essential as a pony. Alice walked back to the stable with her and admired the sleek Daybreak, who took after his father, apart from his stature. Henrietta changed into her riding clothes and left her school skirt hanging on a hook over the manger, where it gathered the straw and dust which stuck to its hem.

Alice said, "Thank you for talking to me."

Henrietta laughed. She climbed the mounting block and slipped into the saddle. "I saw you with Snatchcorn that day. And my father, he was terribly impressed. It's my privilege to speak to you, not the other way round."

It was a strange and pompous thing for the young girl to say, yet it was spoken with such blunt sincerity that Alice was quite overcome, and could think of no answer. Henrietta rode away down the road at a brisk trot towards the gallops behind Heath House and set Daybreak into a flying gallop that took her swiftly out of sight. *What a lovely way to travel to school!*, Alice thought. She went home glowing with happiness at having been recognized. She didn't care about the other girls.

Mrs Scott recognized the change in her and Alice told her all about Henrietta.

Ellen sneered and said, "She's such a clodhopper. Always covered in straw. I wonder Mrs Anstey will have her."

"It's a very respected family," Mrs Scott said. "Her father is a great trainer – you know that perfectly well, Ellen, so don't make fun of Henrietta. She's a tomboy and none the worse for it."

"She's got a wonderful pony," Alice said. But she didn't dare ask for one. Later she thought she would ask Tom if he could think of a way she could get a pony without asking for one.

"Those Scott children have one each and they're hardly used. Can't you use one of those?" Tom asked.

"I want my own," Alice said stubbornly. William's pony was lame and the others too small, except Ellen's, which she wouldn't contemplate riding.

"Maybe your old dad would buy you one," Tom said.

"What, Mr Ticino?"

"Why not? Your proper father paid him off handsomely for old Daisy. What a swap that was – old Daisy, knacker-meat, in exchange for a new gig and a fine young cob to go with it! I reckon he could find a few spare quid from that exchange to fund you a pony. I'll have a word with him."

They were talking leaning over the gate at Paradise – the name had stuck – watching Snatchcorn and Daisy grazing down the field. Alice went there every day, and told Tom things she wouldn't tell Mrs Scott, about how horrid school was. But now she had told him about Henrietta and he said Henrietta's father, Albert Mailer, was a great trainer, better than Mr Scott.

"She'll be a grand friend for you, his Henrietta."

Alice told him about Daybreak. He laughed. Hearing their voices, Snatchcorn and Daisy came up the field. Their winter coats were starting to grow, Snatchcorn's soft and black, like mole fur. He came to Alice, but put his ears back and snapped at Tom. But Tom was able to give him an apple he had in his pocket.

"I'm bribing him, sweetening him like. I'm getting there, slowly. I want him quiet in the stable, but that will be a long road I daresay."

So far, at the end of September, they were still living out, but soon Tom wanted them in at night.

"The sooner you come and live here the better," he said.

"Papa said by Christmas."

The builders were certainly working hard, crashing about all day. Carts were coming and going down the drive, tree fellers hard at work round the gardens. The interior of the house was not too bad and Alice could already see the cleaned and patched rooms turning into something like a home. It was small, but there was only Papa and herself, and William in the holidays. The stables were grand – that's what mattered.

"There is a lot of interest in Snatchcorn now," Tom said.

"Come the spring, the breeders will be queueing up to bring their mares here. I've heard it said on all sides. Your stud will be off to a flying start."

"Papa will be here by then. He said so, for good."

She longed to be here just with Papa. Ellen's malicious presence soured her life at the Scotts', and without William, without Snatchcorn, she found it difficult. When Mrs Scott was around it was all right but Mrs Scott, like most society mothers, was mostly out on her own business or in her own drawing room, leaving her girls to their governess and nanny. Dear Mabel was kept firmly in her place as a servant. Their only chance to talk was at night in their bedrooms. Alice promised Mabel that she would come to Paradise as soon as it was ready. Mabel was thrilled to hear about Henrietta.

"That's the sort of friend you want, not one of the sheep."

Despite her confidence when starting out, poor Mabel was finding life hard at the Scotts' and could hardly keep her eyes open when she came to bed. As she wasn't free till nine, when Alice was usually just about asleep, their conversations were brief.

"Wait till Christmas," Alice said. "When Papa comes home everything will be all right."

To her amazement Tom met her the next day with news from Mr Ticino.

"He says I'm to go to Cambridge market and get you something suitable. Safe, he said."

"Oh Tom!"

How easy it had been after all!

"I'll have a word with Mrs Scott, but we can keep it here. It'll be no trouble for them."

Alice thought of the beautiful Daybreak and said, "Not too safe, Tom. I can ride, after all."

"Leave it to me, Miss Alice."

Alice rushed to school and met Henrietta at the gateway.

"They're going to buy me a pony! I asked! And they said yes!"

"Then we can ride together, and you can visit me," Henrietta said.

Alice had a real friend at last.

When she went to bed she propped the little statue of Goldie up in his place on her pillow and told him she was going to have a real pony.

"But I shall always love you, Goldie, because you introduced me to Snatchcorn. I shall never forget you, even when I have a real pony."

Chapter Ten

After Henrietta started to talk to her, Alice found things much improved at school. Gradually a few of the other girls approached her and started to speak, although a hard core continued to cut her dead. These were mostly the girls she didn't want to be friends with anyway. After a while she was allowed to sit next to Henrietta in the back row, and Miss Pomfret stopped getting red and flustered when she spoke to her. When she put her hand up Miss Pomfret let her answer, although she learned not to do it too often.

"Give the others a chance," Henrietta said.

Henrietta was clever, but chose not to show it. Her life was the horses, and her parents had sent her to school instead of having a governess because they were trying to make her take an interest in the world outside their isolated and busy stable.

"I want to be a trainer," she said. "That's all. I don't want all this." She made a grimace at the pretty surroundings of their school.

"Women can't be trainers," Alice said. But she was going to run a stud, according to her papa.

"I'm going to be a trainer," Henrietta said.

Anything Henrietta said boded to come true. The stern look in her dark eyes and the uncompromising mouth gave her ambition substance. Miss Pomfret accused her of being unwomanly and Henrietta's face lit up at this and she said, "Good." She was ordered to do a hundred lines for insolence. But Henrietta told Alice that her sister would do it for her in exchange for a gallop on Daybreak when their parents weren't looking.

"She's only eight but her writing is very good."

Alice hoped her riding was too. Apparently, as she didn't want to be a trainer, she was allowed to have lessons at home.

"I don't honestly know why my parents want me here. They're quite intelligent otherwise. The only good thing about it is the coming and going."

Then she said, "When's this pony of yours coming?"

Alice was wondering that herself. Tom and Robin had gone to the Cambridge sales and come back empty-handed. Nothing suitable, according to Tom. But they would attend the next sale. Alice was counting the days. She couldn't bear to be disappointed again.

On the day of the next sale, she ran all the way to Paradise after school was over, not even going back with Henrietta to Daybreak's stable as she usually did. Robin was sitting on the driveway gate, waiting for her. Grinning.

"It's lovely," he shouted. "It's called Mother Goose, a grey — well, snow-white actually — fourteen hands high, Irish bred, a little cob, a mare. Pa was going to buy a dreary old thing from a livery yard — safe, he said — and I told him no! I saw this one . . . and it belonged to a girl who had got too big, and I talked to her groom, and he said she was a saint, the pony, I mean, not the girl. And Pa said they all say that and he asked if I could try her — riding, that is — and the groom said yes, so I rode her all around the crowd and she was a saint, never jibbed at a thing. And she was sold with a warranty anyway so Pa said he'd risk it! So it's me that got it for you, Alice, a real cracker she is. Come and look!"

They flew up the drive. Alice's heart was thumping with joy and excitement and her side was killing her with stitch. Tom had already cleared out all the stables, and in the end one stood the neatest little horse Alice had ever seen. Snow white, her mane shaved off but with a tail like a waterfall, she looked like a little charger, ready to do battle. Four-square, wide-chested, she held her head high and looked out with large bright eyes at her new home. When she saw Alice, she gave the same friendly little whicker through her nostrils that Snatchcorn greeted her with.

Alice threw her arms round her neck.

"Oh, you are lovely! My lovely little horse!"

Mother Goose! Alice was entranced. Tom stood by grinning.

"Thank Robin," he said. "A mare, just what we didn't want! But he wouldn't let me buy anything else. I told him it will be his job to keep her clean. It's just a rod for a groom's back, a horse that colour, and his Lordship's two carriage horses the same. Robin will have to do her."

"I don't mind her dirty," Alice cried.

"You'll not have a dirty horse leaving this stable, my girl. I've a reputation to maintain."

"I'll do her," said Robin.

"No, I'll do her," shouted Alice. "Can I have a ride?"

"No, you can't. She's got to settle first."

Alice thought she would burst with happiness. Mother Goose and Snatchcorn – she couldn't wait to tell Henrietta. Not that Mother Goose was much like Daybreak; they couldn't be more different ponies. No Derby winner had come near the parents of Mother Goose.

"If you ride out with that Henrietta, this one'll never keep up with her Daybreak," Tom warned.

"She'll wait for me! She'll wait for me!" Alice shouted.

She was bursting with excitement. She ran home, wishing she had William to tell. And, as if her dreams were all coming true, Mrs Scott said William would be coming home the next weekend, and Ralph was coming too to see how the new building was getting on.

Alice told her about her beautiful new pony and Mrs Scott said, "Thank goodness it sounds like a nice stolid sort. We don't want you breaking your neck before your father gets home. I told Tom, no thoroughbreds."

"She's not a slug, though!" Thank goodness Robin had been there to see her right. An ex-livery-yard carriage horse was not what she wanted. She longed to gallop across the heath with Robin, singing "Gwine to run all day!" Robin was riding out racehorses before school now with a small trainer on the other side of town, but was growing fast and getting more anxious by the day. But Alice wanted him to grow too big so that he couldn't be a "lad", then he would stay and work at Paradise. If Snatchcorn got many mares visiting, they would need more than Tom for the work. She would ask Papa to offer him better wages than Mr Scott.

Ellen said, "I wouldn't be seen dead on a cob."

"You'd look better dead," Alice muttered under her breath.

"Thank goodness it's not cluttering up our stable."

Mrs Scott said to Alice, "We'll drive to Cambridge on Saturday and meet William off the train. You can come with me, Alice, just the two of us. And your father will be here in the evening."

"William never wrote to me," Alice said. "And he said he would."

Mrs Scott said, "No, we only got a few lines, the ones they are ordered to write home. I'm afraid he's not very happy there. People don't write letters if they are unhappy, do they?"

No, Alice supposed they didn't. She never wrote letters at all. She had no one to write them to.

Mrs Scott went on, "It's hard for a boy leaving home for the first time. And boys can be so cruel to each other. He has to get through all that. It's a part of growing up."

Why, Alice wondered? He had a perfectly good tutor at home and could have stayed, couldn't he? But Robin had had some bad times in his riding out job and had told her about it, laughing. But had he laughed at the time, she wondered?

"They held me down in the water trough till I was all but drowned. They emptied their horses' dung in my horse's stable so I had to clear it all out and the guv'nor just about to come on his rounds an' all. And then I got buried in the manure heap lots of times. It's all a bit of fun really, anyone who's new. I join in myself now when it's a new lad."

Alice thought it was probably no worse in its way than Ellen's cruelty to her. Robin was always laughing. The only thing that made him serious was the realization that he was growing too big to be a jockey. Even while Alice commiserated with him, she was secretly pleased, because she wanted him to come with Tom to the new stud.

Tom wouldn't let her ride Mother Goose before the Saturday, sending Robin out on her first to see that she behaved herself when she met the grassy prairie that was Newmarket Heath. Horses unused to such space often went potty on the heath.

But Mother Goose, she learned, was exemplary. "A real lady's ride," said Tom.

Robin whispered, "She can't half go if you ask her!" Alice was thrilled. So by the Saturday of William's arrival she still hadn't ridden her mare, but was harbouring an ambition to have her first ride with Papa on Snatchcorn.

A groom drove Mrs Scott and Alice to Cambridge behind the smart chestnut pair used for the household. They arrived at the station and got out to wait on the platform. It was a cold rainy day with great draughts blowing along the platform. Alice had never been on a train and did not see many, as they went through Newmarket in an underground tunnel so as not to divide the gallops and frighten the horses. She was quite happy looking at everything, but Mrs Scott shivered and said she would go and wait in the carriage.

The train came in and pulled up with much steam and snorting and squealing. Alice looked eagerly for William. There were a lot of schoolboys with servants to meet them, but William came almost last, alone, from the end of the train, carrying a small suitcase.

Alice dashed towards him, then remembered that he wouldn't want to be embarrassed by a girl, and stopped. But she couldn't stop her eyes shining and her voice shouting, "William! William!"

He looked different somehow. Ganglier, whiter, tired. There was no light in his face. He just looked up and smiled and said, "Hey, Alice."

"Oh William!" Alice danced around, trying not to hug him. "Why didn't you write to me? I wanted it so! Your ma's in the carriage outside. No, she's coming, look! Oh, it's so lovely to have you home again! I have missed you so!"

Afterwards she supposed it wasn't really true that she had missed him a lot, because she had seen little of him when she was at Mr Ticino's. But she had certainly thought about him, more than she had thought of anyone. He was her brother. But she didn't kiss him.

Mrs Scott embraced him and he said, "Hullo, Mother," and that's all.

They got in the carriage and William sat next to Mrs Scott with Alice opposite and the groom started to weave the horses away through the traffic.

And then, to Alice's amazement, William burst into tears and let out a terrible wail. He turned to Mrs Scott and she put her arms out and he buried his face into her astrakhan chest and sobbed bitterly. Mrs Scott hugged him, rocking him slightly, holding her cheek against his hair.

"There," she said. "There, it's all right. It's all right."

Her face was twisted with love and grief, and trying not to cry herself.

William would not stop. Alice, horrified, started to cry too, looking out of the window. The horses were out of the worst of the traffic and the grey shops were speeding past. Their little crying world whirled out of Cambridge. By the time they were out in the country William's sobs had subsided somewhat and Alice had stopped hers by sheer willpower.

"Ladies don't cry in public," Miss Pomfret had instructed.

Alice didn't want William to think she had noticed. But obviously he knew she had, for when he came up out of Mrs Scott's bosom he looked across blotchily and said, "Sorry. Think nothing of it," and gave a watery sort of smile.

Alice went on looking out of the window.

Her heart was beating so hard she had to bite her lip and strive to keep calm. Seeing William washed up like that with those comforting arms round him and Mrs Scott's loving face pressed against his had prompted in her the memory of the dream of the lady in red velvet and jewels holding out her arms and calling her "My Alice". It came back as clearly as if she had just woken up and gave her such a jolt that she thought she was back in her old bedroom at Mr Ticino's.

She stared out of the window, trying to bring herself back to earth. She hadn't got a mother.

But when she looked at William he grinned and she managed to grin back, coming back to the present. He said, "Sorry about that. Don't tell anyone."

"No, of course not. Nobody at all."

"A few tears are nothing to be ashamed of," said Mrs Scott briskly. "Homesickness can be a terrible thing."

Her face was quite as usual now. Alice wondered if she had seen that look after all.

Did everyone cover up feelings like that?

Was it something ladies and gentlemen did?

By the time they got home William was himself again. She was afraid he might avoid her, having been witness to such emotion, but he actually sought her out in her room and sat on her bed and said, "How's things? I hear our father is coming home tonight."

"Yes. For all he said he was going to live in Newmarket, he's not started yet. I wish he would."

"He's waiting for the house to be ready, isn't he?"

"Yes, I suppose so. After Christmas," he said.

She told him about school and Henrietta and Mother Goose.

"School was dreadful at first, just like you said it would be. No one spoke to me. But then Henrietta did, and after that it was all right. Did you find out at your school who our mother is?"

"No. Of course they said she was a prostitute, but I know that's not true."

"What's a prostitute?"

"You'll find out when you're older."

"I am older."

"Older still."

"So is school really horrible?"

"Unspeakably horrible. I can't tell you how horrible. If I have to go back, I think I'll run away."

"Run here. I'll hide you."

"Maybe."

"Is it Papa that makes you go? Or were you going to go anyway?"

"Oh, most boys go, I suppose. I knew it was going to happen. My tutor said I must go. And I suppose the worst must be over."

But he did not sound convinced.

"You won't tell Papa about . . . you know. Or that I've said anything?" William was anxious now. "I'll tell him it's not bad."

"No. Not a word."

Alice was warmed by William's company. It made her feel as if she belonged — where, she was not sure, but he was family. Real. They were both on pins waiting for their father to arrive, and when the carriage was sent to the station to meet him, they both went with it. This time the train arrival brought nothing but joy and excitement. He appeared out of the throng as eager and excited as they were and hugged them both. A porter brought his luggage and they piled into the carriage. But the journey was so short they had no time to say anything important, and then he was received by the Scotts and they had to take a back seat. At dinner the talk was of racing. Alice sat sighing, swinging her legs under the table. How she longed to leave this place for Paradise, where she would have Papa and Snatchcorn all to herself!

But in the morning all was well. The Scott family went to church but Ralph said, "God will forgive us if we go to Paradise instead."

They walked. It only took fifteen minutes. Alice supposed her father was really coming to see how the house was getting on, but the house took second place to the horses. Mother Goose was duly admired, and then Snatchcorn was caught up and stood for inspection by Tom. Tom was learning to handle the horse without getting hurt, but it wasn't an easy job.

"Old habits die hard," he said.

"I can see a great improvement," Ralph said. "You've done well. But he needs to be exercised now, to get him muscled up. Breeders won't want to see a stallion at grass."

Tom looked doubtful. "I can lunge him, sir, but I don't fancy riding him. I'm no rider."

"I'll start riding him when I move in. But meanwhile – yes, start lungeing him. And maybe that boy of yours, Robin, is he a good rider?"

"I can't say how good, sir. He stays on."

"We'll have to talk about employing him when he leaves school, unless he's set on being a jockey. Alice tells me that's his ambition."

"Yes, sir, but he's growing fast. I doubt he'll stay light enough. I would like him to have a job here."

Alice was delighted by this conversation. She capered after Will and her father to the house after Snatchcorn had been put back in his field. She realized that she had taken very little interest in what the builders had been doing. She was amazed at the progress.

"Why, it's ready to live in!"

She had been aware of a huge posse of builders at work, but had never stopped to see what they were doing. Now, as they pushed open the front door, they found themselves in a large, square hall with a fine staircase rising up before them. On either side were beautiful rooms with long doors opening out on to the cleared lawns, and down some stairs and through a door to the left there was a brand-new kitchen with the most up-to-date range and cooker, and plenty of room for a table and chairs in the middle. How Mrs Pinney would have loved it! It put poor Mr Ticino's skinny kitchen to shame. Alice, having lived most of her life in Mr Ticino's kitchen, saw at once what a splendid place this would be. The door opened, most appropriately, straight into the stable-yard. Tom and Robin could come in and have their tea here!

"Oh, how fine it is!"

Upstairs there was a bedroom for her looking down into the stable-yard, a bedroom and study for William with tall bookcases already in place, a large bedroom for Ralph and a spare one at the end. And up another smaller flight of stairs were rooms in the attic for the servants, not poky at all, but all with pleasant dormers looking out over the lawns. William looked all around but made no comment.

"Oh, it's a lovely house!" Alice shouted. "When can we move in?"

"By Christmas," Ralph said. "The builders promised. I shall move some furniture up from London and my old cook, Mrs Carstairs, will move up here with her husband. You will like her, Alice, she is an old dear, and wants an easier life than she gets in London."

"And can Mabel come? Please ask Mrs Scott!"

"Certainly; we shall need a housemaid, and a manservant. If you want Mabel I'm sure that can be arranged."

"It is Paradise," Alice said solemnly. "Truly."

To be here with Papa and William and Tom and Robin and Mabel and Snatchcorn and Mother Goose, with Henrietta to visit, and no Ellen . . . yes, it was her idea of paradise.

And then William said bluntly to his father, "When you come to live here, will you be alone?"

There was a sudden, strange silence. Alice knew what William meant, the question she dared not ask herself. They had a home now: it was all coming together, except that of the main player there was no word.

William said, "I think we ought to know."

Alice could see that it was very difficult for him to say this. His face was pale and strained and showed quite clearly the miseries he had been suffering. Ralph walked out of the hall and stood on the front doorstep, looking out over the cleared ground. It was very quiet, the church bells having ceased, and the day being still and silent, a perfect November morning. The sun was chasing away a faint mist and large golden leaves fluttered idly down from the chestnut trees accompanied by the soft intermittent thud of conkers. The sweet smell of turned earth and distant muck heaps hung in the air. It struck Alice suddenly how very young their father looked.

"Yes, you ought to know, it's true. Will it be enough, now, for you to know that at Christmas you will meet your mother? But whether she will come to live here with us – I can't say."

Neither Alice nor William could find anything to say. They were both stunned.

"It is my dearest wish in all the world that she will, and my deepest fear that she won't. So if you feel that I am not much of a father, that my mind is often far away, you are quite right. I am thinking of her all the time. But after Christmas, when

162

the future will be decided, then – whatever happens – I will come back here and be a good father. For ever and ever, amen."

And he looked at their amazed faces and smiled.

Chapter Eleven

"So who is your mother?" Henrietta asked.

"I don't know."

"People say—" Henrietta hesitated.

"What do people say?"

"Well, the odd thing is, most of the toffs that come here for the racing – a lot of them bring ladies – ladies that aren't necessarily their wives, and people know what goes on . . . like the Prince of Wales and his lady friends . . . that sort of thing. But about your father, everyone knows he has never married. He has never been seen with a woman, but he takes it for granted that everyone knows you and your brother are his children and nobody – *nobody* – knows who the lady is. The trainers call him Lord Mystery. It's really weird."

"Really?" This was news to Alice. She wasn't sure anyway what "that sort of thing" meant and would have to refer this conversation to Mabel, as usual.

She was riding Mother Goose at the time of this conversation, and Henrietta was on Daybreak. It was a winter Saturday morning, and the ride was for pleasure. They met halfway and did a tour of the gallops, taking in the racehorses at exercise, all of which Henrietta recognized and could name. Alice was very jealous of this knowledge and was trying hard to learn it for herself. Riding with Henrietta was the best part of the week, even if she couldn't keep up with Daybreak. But riding Mother Goose, even if she couldn't gallop as fast, was pure heaven. The little mare was so sparky and keen and yet so easy to ride, never feeling like bolting or bucking. She could be trusted utterly. Alice had never pretended to be a great rider, although she could see that Henrietta was one. Henrietta sat like Papa, part of the horse, so still and confident. And Daybreak was full of tricks and fire, not easy at all. Alice had no desire for a ride on Daybreak.

They walked slowly back down the hill towards town. Henrietta liked to come and visit Snatchcorn, for whom she had as great an admiration as Alice did.

"But if you are going to meet your mother – like he says – you will find out who she is and you can tell everybody," Henrietta said. "And if he brings her back here – the mystery will be solved."

"But why now? When it's been a secret ever since I was born? Something must have happened to change it. Why couldn't we have met her ages ago?"

"Mystery indeed!" Henrietta was intrigued. "How strange to meet your mother when you're eleven!"

"Twelve," said Alice, having had a birthday.

"And is he bringing her back here to live?"

"He said he might. And then he might not."

"Mysteriouser and mysteriouser."

Alice longed to have a mother to hand. To go to church with. To meet her out of school. To make it all right with the beastly ladies who cut her dead. Since leaving Mr Ticino's her world had become full of strange rebuffs, uncertainties and surprises. But Henrietta was her staunch friend and the best thing that had happened to her.

They caught Snatchcorn and gave him carrots, and then Alice showed Henrietta over the house to show her how beautiful it was, and then Henrietta rode off for her gallop home. Alice walked back to the Scotts' in time for lunch.

Mrs Scott said her father sent word that as soon as William came home from school again, for Christmas, they were to be sent to London. He would meet them at St Pancras.

"To meet your mother. Just imagine that – at last!" Mrs Scott seemed as excited as Alice felt.

Ellen was sending her daggers across the lunch table, jealous of the attention she would certainly command in Newmarket if she appeared with a real mother. Alice felt tingly all over at the thought.

The great mystery was to be unravelled at last.

William arrived home in a slightly less despondent state the next time, two weeks before Christmas. He said he still didn't want to go back, especially if he could live and work in his ripping new study at Paradise, but he thought Papa would want him to. He looked even thinner and paler than before and said being useless at games put him at a big disadvantage.

"It's really odd, but being clever – which I am – doesn't go down well at all. But if you can kick a ball it makes you really respected. How can that be logical?"

"I'm clever too, and they don't like it," said Alice.

"It'll count when we're old, though, I bet," William said.

They had to take comfort in that.

"Is it better, though?"

"Fractionally," said William. "There's a chap I can talk to. Just one."

"Like me and Henrietta," Alice said.

Mrs Scott took them to Cambridge to buy new clothes.

William said to Alice, "We've got to look smart for our mother. To make her want to come and live with us, we've got to look desirable. We're going as bait – the sort of children a mother would like to have."

"That's a horrid thing to say."

But perhaps it was true. Alice tried to think of it from her mother's point of view, meeting her children for the first time when they were twelve years old. Really odd. One would like them to be handsome, upstanding and well-dressed, obviously, not scruffy, spotty, ugly and dull. A bit like the sale ring in Newmarket, where the crackers got snapped up and the splay-footed, weak-jointed, dull-skinned beasts went out unsold.

Alice had never been on a train before, let alone to London. It was one of the most exciting things, apart from taming

Snatchcorn, that she had ever done in her life. William knew all about trains, of course, and sat unconcerned while Alice sat looking out of the window trying not to shout with excitement at the things she saw whizzing past. It was extraordinary, how fast they whizzed. And then, when they were nearly there, the grey rows and rows of houses and factories and smoke and dirt and roads full of horse traffic below them, steaming and sweating, like a hundred Cambridges all rolled together, on and on. If this was London it was horrid.

"Is this London?" she asked William in amazement. "Is this where our father lives?"

"There are much nicer bits. It's not all like this," William said. "You'll see."

Such noise and hubbub! The station was filled with smoke, which made her eyes smart. A porter took their luggage and they trailed along behind him until they saw their father appear out of the murk. He gave them great hugs and swept them and their luggage out to the street where the lovely white horses were waiting for them, coachman and groom all ready to help. Poor horses, weaving their way through traffic such as Alice had never seen, wheel to wheel, stopping, starting, carts of every size, buses, mail coaches, gigs and traps, smart pairs like theirs and hansoms everywhere. How could people live like this?

She sat staring out of the window. The cobbled streets were carpeted with horse dung, which poor men tried to sweep away in places – what a job! They went past the Bank of

England – Papa pointed it out – they caught a glimpse of St Paul's, then moved down along Holborn – all places and names she had heard of from books and pictures.

William looked out idly, obviously used to these changes of scene. Alice knew she was a country bumpkin and it was impossible not to let it show, although she did her best. The streets were so grand, full of business and shops. Where did people live?

But at last the horses turned down a quieter street, and then into a beautiful square with trees all round, and shining white houses with steps up to the front doors and black railings along the pavement. The carriage pulled up and their father said, "Here we are. This is my London house."

They got out and servants came running out to take their luggage. Up the steps and into a beautiful hall Alice went, gaping and amazed, escorted by a butler and a housekeeper all in black, smiling and welcoming. Pictures of racehorses gazed down at her from every wall, clocks chimed, fires flickered cheerfully beneath carved marble mantelpieces, thick carpets padded their steps. It was Paradise again, in London style. *This is my father's house*, thought Alice. *This is my house! I live here. Me. Alice Ticino*. Except she wasn't Ticino any more, was she? Her head was spinning.

"Do you like it?" Her father was smiling.

"It's beautiful!"

"One day you will be pleased to have a house in London. When you are older and want to go to balls."

"I don't want to go to balls!"

He considered her, serious, and said, "No, perhaps not. You are going to run my stud in Newmarket with its valuable stallion whose life you saved, and what are balls in London compared to that?"

Exactly, thought Alice. Her father understood.

But William said, very sensible, "She could come to a ball or two as well run a stud in Newmarket."

"Of course. Work and play, you're quite right, William." And he laughed.

They were shown to their bedrooms, and had a late lunch in the dining room, waited on by footmen. Alice couldn't help staring, although she tried not to. Men in uniform to hand the vegetables! Amazing! They stood against the wall, staring into space, while the three of them ate at the table, then leapt to pass the dishes, or gather them up. Even at the Scotts' it had only been a maid and that butler. And at home old Pinney . . . (Pinney seemed so far away now!)

But the reason for their being there, to meet their mother, overlaid even this novelty with an air of tension that became almost suffocating as time crept on. They finished the meal and went into the sitting room and Ralph said to them, "We will be going out at six. Be sure you're ready." He left them.

It was a relief to be alone together. They sat on a gilt sofa beside the fire and tried to feel optimistic.

"What do you think she's like?"

"She might be just ordinary," William said.

"She might be a duchess!"

"Or a cancan dancer."

"Why can't she come and be our mother anyway? Why hasn't she been, all along? Why did she give us away?"

"Because she's married to someone else, twaddle-head. That's obvious."

"Will we meet him too?"

"No, of course not. We're a secret."

"A scandal, you said."

"Yes, a scandal."

"I do so want her to come home. I want a mother. It's different for you, because you've got Mrs Scott. I've never had anyone."

"I know. It's hard cheese. But it's quite nice as it is, just him and us. Don't you think so? He's a really decent chap. Much nicer than most fathers."

"Yes." It was true. But a really decent mother to go with him would be . . . Alice shivered . . . what she had dreamed of all her life! But what would William know about her feelings in that direction?

"I want. . ."

Impossible. Those arms round her in that dream – "My Alice! My darling Alice!" Seeing William weep with his head buried in Mrs Scott's bosom, that was what she wanted. It made her tremble to think of, that it might be going to happen. Might be.

When Ralph came back at half-past five they were ready

and waiting in their outdoor clothes. A friendly young maid had combed Alice's hair for her and put the ribbons back in and they had squashed her best hat on top and stuck it down with pins so that it all looked tidy. Her hat was dark brown velvet with cream roses at the side, and her best winter outfit was cream with brown lacings and very smart, and her muff was of dark fur, very cosy. She looked as good as possible, she thought, considering the material. She seemed to be growing out of clothes quite fast lately, and was the same height as William now, so that they did really look like twins. Their mother was surely going to approve!

"We'll walk there; it's not far," their father said.

They walked in silence, quickly, through the squares now all lit with gas lamps. The pavements were busy and hansoms and carriages trotted past, lamps twinkling on their sides. Nannies in uniform hurried home with their perambulators; a man sold hot chestnuts from a brazier. The air was thick with the smell of smoke which plumed up from all the chimneys, hazing the stars and the half-moon which hung in the bare branches of the plane trees in the square gardens. There was a Christmas atmosphere in the sharp air, and glimpses of decorations and candlelit Christmas trees through the tall, elegant windows of the town houses.

I live here! thought Alice, and couldn't help a skip.

But she remembered what they were about, and her heart began to thump uncomfortably. Her father was silent and pale, tight-lipped. What did it all mean to him? Alice couldn't begin to guess. Save that she thought it was worse for him, as bad as it could be.

The house was larger and grander than his.

Certainly not a cancan dancer, far more likely a duchess.

A footman in livery took their coats. Getting her hat off took Alice ages but he stood stony-faced while she wrestled with the pins and he gave a little bow as she handed it over. As she glanced up and saw her father watching her, unsmiling, she realized suddenly that he was as handsome and lovely a man as any she had ever seen and no lady in her right mind could possibly leave him. *Nor leave me!* she thought.

And they then followed a butler across the hall and into a small study where he indicated they were to wait. The walls were lined with books and a big fire burned in the grate. It was homely more than smart, with a large, well-used sofa covered in gold brocade, and two leather armchairs on either side of the fire. Alice and William sat on the sofa side by side. Their father stood in front of the fire. Nobody spoke.

They heard footsteps hurrying outside, and then the door opened and she came in.

Her gaze flew to their father, then to Alice and William. And Alice realized at once that, even if she had thought she was suffering, it was nothing to the agony that showed in her mother's face.

She came across to the sofa where William had stood up and Alice just sat staring. Her mother was beautiful. She had gorgeous red-brown hair heaped in curls over her forehead and she wore crimson velvet and sparkling pearls and diamonds exactly as in Alice's long-remembered dream. And as in the dream her arms stretched out in welcome and she cried out, "My Alice, my darling Alice!"

The words Alice had never forgotten. She leapt up and fell into the encircling arms. Exactly as in her dream, just like William and Mrs Scott! Her mother held her as if she would never let her go, burying her face in Alice's hair and saying over and over, "My Alice, my darling Alice!" They both wept. Alice felt the hot tears coming as if out of a tap.

William stood by, acutely embarrassed, hoping he wasn't going to get the same treatment. But no. Although she embraced him in his turn, it was a far less emotional welcome, the sort one could cope with at public school.

"Dear William! How handsome you are, just like your father!"

And then they were all standing together and laughing, their father too, the white pinched look gone from his face. Staring . . . Alice could not take her eyes off this wonderful woman, her mother.

She was quite small, with porcelain-white skin and huge dark eyes, violet shadowed. No wrinkles at all, very young-looking like Papa. Her hair was wild, like Alice's, but expertly coiffed, no doubt by a good maid, except for the curling tendrils that had escaped during their enthusiastic embrace. Alice thought she could see it flying loose in a great cloud as she galloped over Newmarket Heath with her father. Had they? Would they again?

Alice groaned with the joy and the longing that went with it, not taking her eyes off her, and then laughing because she was so beautiful. Who was she? Alice had no idea.

A maid brought tea on a silver tray and set it down, unnoticed.

"Sit down, sit down!" ordered their mother, and they sat in a circle round the low tea table before the fire.

She poured.

"I just want to enjoy you, look at you," she said. "My twins! My own children! How I have longed for this, I cannot tell you!"

The tea went all over the tray-cloth and their father gently took the teapot from her and said, "You look, and I'll pour."

They all laughed.

"I can't believe it," she said. "How like your father you are! Everyone must have noticed."

"No," said Alice. Even she hadn't.

"And I heard all about your taming the stallion, Alice. How that pleased your father! You have his love of horses, mine too. How splendid! And I hear you are very clever, William, and that you hate school. I don't want you to go back if you don't like it. It is so cruel."

"I don't mind," lied William, reddening up.

"They say it does you good," she said dubiously. "Certainly it sets you up in life, meeting everyone. But, well, it is for you to decide with your father. It gets better, they always say."

"Yes, it gets better," Papa said.

William had said this to Alice, saying it must do so because it couldn't possibly get worse, so he agreed politely.

"Life is not always how you want it to be," said their mother, and she looked at Papa and tears came into her eyes again. But then she tossed her head and laughed.

"How stupid we are, to get into such tangles! And you, Alice, you have been so uncomplaining all these years, when your father and I made such a bungle of looking after you. Not looking after you, rather. With that sinister Mr Ticino. His wife Rose was a dear, you see, and wanted a child so badly, and loved you so much. She was an orphan, poor dear, and had no relatives of her own, and had married Mr Ticino out of desperation, I think. I went abroad and when I came back I heard she had died! I was so upset, but Mr Ticino said he loved you and you were being very well looked after, which Mrs Scott told me was true, so I am afraid I didn't enquire more closely. I couldn't bear it, to see you again and have another parting! I thought I should die of it. I wanted so much for Mrs Scott to have you too, so that you could be with your brother, but she was ill at that time and quite unable to take on another child, and Mr Scott didn't want another girl. He said they had too many already. And besides, for various reasons, it was impossible for me to visit you. I am not free to do as I want, you see. I have never been free, I'm afraid. Nor am I now."

And she looked at their father with such fierceness, a mix of longing and defiance, that Alice saw that he would have no say in the matter as to what was going to happen. For all she was small she had a fiery spirit that seemed to radiate out of her: she would command, and they would obey. Alice stared at her with open admiration and love: this was her mother! Alice, having been prepared in her heart for disappointment – how could anyone live up to her expectations? – now found that yes, her mother not only lived up to her expectations, but surpassed them.

(Afterwards she supposed that she was biased and saw it all through a rosy haze but, comparing notes with William, she found that he agreed and said, "No, she was amazing. Hypnotic. No wonder he's never found anyone else to love, having had her. No one else could possibly match up." And William was never one to exaggerate.)

"Now tell me about Snatchcorn and your new pony, and William must tell me how horrid Rugby is and we'll try and decide what to do about it."

So the fraught moment passed and they chatted, drawn out by her sympathy. Papa did not say much, but just watched and listened, a spectator. He was very pale and looked so drawn and ill. *Don't say he was going to die of love!* thought Alice. People did, in books.

She scarcely remembered any of the rest of the conversation, although she chattered away nineteen to the dozen. No adult she had ever met had listened with such attention and sympathy. And William too became quite animated, serious boy that he was, and even laughed about Rugby, as if it didn't matter. And Papa just sat there, watching.

And then a footman came in with a message, which he delivered in a soft voice to their mother, and all the animation went out of her face. She stood up.

"You've got to go, children," she said.

And the embrace came again, those soft arms and the wonderful scent, and her mother's tears raining down to mingle with Alice's own: "I can't bear it, oh Alice, my darling girl! I am so sorry, I am so sorry for how it is!" Their wild hair fell out of its pins, mingling, and Alice's last glimpse of her mother stayed in her mind as the figure of a child like herself, dishevelled and tear-stained, in spite of the velvet gown and the sparking jewellery. And Papa going to her and standing there with his arm round her, holding her close. And then they were out in the street with another footman to escort them home, because Papa was staying longer, and flakes of snow were falling out of the sky like tears, just as her own.

"Oh William! She's not coming, is she? Else she wouldn't have cried so!"

"No. Hail and farewell, it seemed like."

They scurried after the long-striding footman through the squares, unseeing.

"Who is she – and why can't she come?"

"Papa will tell us, I daresay. The secret's out, now we've met her, isn't it? He'll have to say."

"She's so beautiful and lovely!"

"Yes. Strange, isn't it, having a mother like that? I never thought, well, I thought probably pretty and sort of soppy like mothers are, you know, but she . . . she . . ." Words failed him.

"She was strong!"

"She was like you."

"No! I'm not like her at all. Don't be stupid."

William shrugged. "I'm glad she . . . she was all right. Not a let-down. I was scared."

"Me too."

Meeting her had bonded the two of them, too, in a way they both recognized but could not speak of. For the first time in her whole life Alice was aware of being part of a family. In spite of the fresh grief of parting, there was a warmth spreading all through her as if the sun was suddenly shining out of the night sky. The snowflakes were rose petals, the icy wind zephyrs of summer. She laughed and skipped. She belonged.

"Oh William, she's lovely! Lovely!"

And he laughed too.

And then he said, "She's not coming, though. You could tell."

"No."

And they both said in the same breath, "Poor Papa."

He came home quite late. They weren't in bed, as there was nobody to tell them to go. They were sitting by the fire talking. They heard Papa dismiss the butler, and the butler say that the children were still up, sir, and he came in. He looked like a ghost, Alice thought, gaunt and wild with snowflakes in his hair and wet on his cheeks. Or were they tears? Did men cry? Alice didn't think they did. William stood up and she did too, feeling very small and inadequate, wishing she had gone to bed.

"I shouldn't have brought you here," he said, "to raise your expectations. She is going away."

"We guessed she wasn't coming, sir," William said, in a soothing voice.

"But much better that we came," Alice said stoutly, "and met her, even if she is going away."

"It makes it all so much worse, for her too. I thought, if she met you, she might not be able to go. But she is so strong. I never realized how strong."

"Where's she going?" Alice asked.

"Russia."

"Russia!" Alice had rather thought Ireland or Paris, somewhere not very far.

"Her husband is an ambassador, and she says it is her duty to go, otherwise the scandal would be too terrible for him and his life would be ruined. Which is true, of course."

"But she loves you!"

"Yes. But she is very loyal, and has a strong sense of duty. She is right. I am wrong. It isn't possible for her to come and live with us. I was stupid to think it was possible. As they say, love is blind."

"Who is her husband, sir?" William asked.

"Her husband?" He gave a name which even Alice recognized, the name of a high-ranking politician, a friend of the queen's, a world-famous diplomat.

"It is true that if she left him his life would be in ruins. In our hypocritical society one can have affairs and liaisons as long the outward appearances are kept up, the charade maintained. She only agreed to meet you because – even if the secret of who your mother is now comes out in Newmarket – it no longer matters. They will no longer be on the scene, having to keep up appearances. They will be in Russia and her husband's job is secure and the scandal won't touch them out there."

"Why did she marry him if she loved you?" Alice asked.

"She married him when she was very young. He is much older than she is. It was a marriage of convenience, arranged by her parents for financial reasons. You probably don't know anything about this sort of thing, but it is very prevalent in high-born families. It's their way of life."

"But you have a title and lots of money!" Alice cried. "She could have married you!'

"No, I'm only a minnow amongst the aristocracy, Alice, a tiny fish, not worth considering. And besides, she was married when we first met. It was all too late. Of course she never loved him, but he is a kind man. He has always been good to her, even when she had you children, which he knew were not his. I can see that she cannot leave him. She is absolutely right, and I am an idiot to think she might have come. I am an idiot."

"I don't think so," Alice said. "If you want something so badly, you have to try, don't you?"

"I'm sorry she's not coming, but I'm glad we met her, sir, all the same," William said.

"So am I!" Alice said. "It was wonderful! Now we know who she is and what she's like."

"I'm ashamed that you have been brought up in such ignorance. It is your right to know these things. I am so sorry . . . so sorry. . ."

"But it's been all right up to now," Alice pointed out. "Only lately it's been a muddle. And now it's all right again, since you came."

William said, "If her husband is a lot older than she is, she might come when he dies."

"Oh yes!" shouted Alice. "He might die in Russia, of the cold. Or get run down by a . . . a. . ." What were they called? ". . . a *troika*!"

"Alice! Really!" But her father smiled, all the same. "Yes, if she were free she would come. So we can but live in hope. Although I suppose we mustn't wish the old boy dead. It's very cruel."

"How old is he?" Alice asked.

"Nearly seventy, I think. And quite blameless. We mustn't wish him ill."

No, thought Alice, *not out loud. But in our private prayers . . . a kindly death. . .* She would start tonight.

"And now I think it's time you were in bed. And tomorrow

we will go back to Newmarket and think about Christmas. And the stud, because the mares will start coming to visit Snatchcorn and we must be prepared."

He brightened slightly, and they kissed him goodnight and went to their rooms.

But not to sleep, certainly. The vision went round and round in Alice's head – the mother of her dreams made flesh, hugging her. She could still feel those arms and the soft fur of the velvet and the white cheek; she could feel her mother's heart beating against her own. Her mother! How she loved to say those words! Even if she never saw her again, Alice knew that she was loved, would always be loved, and had even been loved when she was a baby by poor Mrs Ticino. What riches to nurse her starved ego! *I am loved! I am loved!*

And the hard lump under her pillow that was Goldie did not feel her reaching hand that night, nor ever again.

Chapter Twelve

When they returned to Newmarket, they arrived at Paradise to find Mr and Mrs Carstairs already installed, and the contents of four large horse-drawn pantechnicons disgorged into the hall and the various rooms. There was furniture, carpets, curtains, paintings – everything to set up the house. Best of all, Mabel had come to help.

"Mrs Scott has released me to come and work here! Your wonderful papa prevailed on her. And Mrs Carstairs is an old dear, much sweeter than Mrs Pinney and the Scotts' housekeeper, who did her best to make my life a misery."

Alice hugged her, but Mabel pushed her away.

"None of that now! You've got to behave like a lady, remember – I'm here to keep an eye on you, see you're brought up proper!"

Lady or not, Alice helped get the house straight, with William and Papa helping too. They wanted to live in it straightaway, and all the furniture had to be put in the right places. The pantechnicon men carried all the big pieces into place. Outside it started to snow, and the pantechnicon horses wore waterproof rugs and had their nosebags put on, waiting patiently. Alice directed the arrangement of her room, and was entranced by the beautiful curtains Papa provided of embroidered silk, with exotic birds flying all over them and a silken counterpane to match. Best of all was the view from the window of Snatchcorn brought in out of the snow, looking contentedly out of the top door of his loose box in the yard. Alice always handled him when she was at home, although Tom could manage now without getting more than snapped at. The horse was mellowing.

Getting the house together took their minds off the events in London. Sometimes Alice wondered if it had been a dream, meeting their mother. The journey and the wonderful houses had been like a dream, and the ambience of their mother's rooms, the stately servants, the soft, exotic aura of great wealth and luxury – Alice found it hard to relate to. After a lifetime in Mrs Pinney's cold kitchen it was hard to believe that she truly belonged in that London world of wealth and status. Papa said it need no longer be a secret who her mother was, now that she was far away in St Petersburg, out of the range of gossiping tongues.

"After St Petersburg her husband will retire out of public life, and the scandal will not harm him. Our secrets need be secrets no longer."

So boo-sucks to Ellen, Alice thought, *and those dreadful boys at William's school*.

If Papa did not want to keep the secret any longer, no doubt the cutting parents would know it as quickly as the winter wind scattered the golden leaves in the first Christmas storms. Mabel would be able to tell her the state of current gossip, day by day. Maybe she would return to school a heroine. Maybe! It made no difference to Henrietta. In fact she was rather disappointed. "I thought she might be an actress, you know, like Sarah Bernhardt, or an opera singer or something. But someone in politics . . . well—"

"Her husband's in politics, not her."

"Well, politics is all secrets, everyone knows that. And terribly boring."

"Yes." (Although, to Alice, St Petersburg did sound rather exotic and elegant.)

Mabel was right about Mrs Carstairs being an old dear, very free with the biscuits and raisins, and the maker of wonderful cakes and sweetmeats. She loved her new home. "So peaceful! And such an easy house, none o' them stairs up to the dining room and down to the cellars. Have another gingerbread man, my darling. Your dear papa loved gingerbread men when he was a little lad. He used to come into my kitchen and steal them."

She was making Christmas cakes and puddings all day long.

"Rather late, I'm afraid, but no doubt they'll get eaten."

Mr Carstairs was a little quiet man who cleaned the silver and the shoes and brought the coal in and sawed logs and did the garden – or would do the garden when spring came. He was very kind. He made tiny posies of leaves and rose hips and an early snowdrop to put on Alice's dressing table. Alice had never met such consideration before. Mrs Carstairs said he had taught her father to ride when he was a little boy. "Mr Carstairs was head groom in the big house when he was young, in charge of the hunters. That's when I met him, when I was just a housemaid." Alice realized that there was a mine of information awaiting her in the kitchen which would keep her entertained for many a winter's day.

But for now getting the house ready for Christmas was a full-time job. They had moved in, and big fires were lit in every room to dry the house out, and Mrs Scott came over to see that their sheets were aired properly and the hot water system was performing as it should, and to make sure that Mrs Carstairs was as efficient as Ralph said she was. She was impressed on every score.

"It's a credit to you, I'm sure. I never saw the possibilities in the old ruin, I must say. I never believed it could turn out so well."

Alice could see that she was relieved to have her own home to herself again, to save worrying over Ellen's aggression. She knew about their meeting their mother, but did not speak of it. It was too difficult.

Alice gave a thought to poor old Mrs Pinney still labouring alone in Mr Ticino's bleak house and looking after her terrible old mother. She spoke to Papa about it, rather anxiously.

He said, "Well, she made a good job of bringing you up. Perhaps she deserves some comfort in her old age –

retirement and a cottage of her own. I will see to it, Alice. You are right to remind me."

Alice had been thinking a nice Christmas present. A cottage of her own – poor old Pinney would die of excitement! Generally the old Mrs Pinneys of the world went into the workhouse if they had no family to look after them. Mrs Pinney had no family that Alice knew of. What a good idea to give her her own little house!

"Your papa is a kind man and no mistake," Mabel said.

And, even more surprising, Mr Ticino called to see how the house had turned out, having been the estate agent involved in its purchase, and he stayed talking for some time. Once again he smiled and looked quite human, and after that first visit he called at intervals and stayed for a drink. When he left he chucked Alice under the chin and called her poppet.

It was Christmas day. At last!

"Gwine to run all night!
Gwine to run all day!"

They shouted at the tops of their voices, Alice and Robin, galloping up the heath on Mother Goose and Daisy. There wasn't a soul in sight. It was like being on the moon. Alice's hair had come loose and was flying in the wind, catching snowflakes. She could hear the church bells from All Saints, but it was early, scarcely light. Church was not for ages! William was still in bed snoring and Papa – Papa was out of sight. Papa was mad.

"You can't ride Snatchcorn!" she had shouted at him.

"Can't I?" he shouted back, and had the saddle on in a trice.

"Bring Daisy," he shouted back over his shoulder as he rode away, "else she'll kick the stable down!"

"I want to come on Mother Goose! Robin can ride Daisy!"

"Quick, saddle them up!" she shouted at Robin and ran indoors to scramble into her habit, and then they were away, the two of them like old times, singing their songs. Snatchcorn was a dot in the distance on the sea of mown grass that rose up from the town.

Alice lifted her head up into the wind and saw the big steely Christmas clouds rolling in from the east, straight from Siberia, but the bitter cold could not compete with the warmth in her being. She was so happy!

> "I bet my money on a bobtail nag,
> Somebody bet on de bay!"

Robin was full of spirits. He had already done his stable lad work with the racehorses, fed and mucked out, but on Christmas day there was no riding. He had the rest of the day off. He was going fishing.

"You're crazy," Alice said, "fishing on Christmas day!"

When they were together, on the horses, it was just as if

they were still the two of them in Mr Ticino's stables in town, shouting and teasing. Robin was the cheerful lad he had always been, just larger now. Almost as good as a brother, like William. Save she had to remember he was a servant, Mabel said. Mabel was getting just like Mrs Pinney. Alice still wasn't quite sure why that made a difference. He was really nice, which was what mattered.

Snatchcorn was coming back now, pirouetting down the gallops. Alice's father sat easily in the saddle, very relaxed. Alice saw again what a fine rider he was. When he reached them he looked slightly shame-faced and said, "I shouldn't have done that, on an unfit horse. But my word, he wanted it too! What a feel he gives you! What a star he is!"

"My father said you used to ride him when he was racing," Robin said.

"I did indeed. I only wished I could have ridden him in a race! But he was a baby then. He feels like a real horse now, so powerful. I shall ride him out and keep him fit – such a waste not to use him."

Alice thought it was really Christmas now, riding with Papa on the heath. Snatchcorn looked magnificent in his mole-dark winter coat, now rimmed with sweat, his flared nostrils sending clouds into the cold morning. He arched his stallion crest and tossed the too-long mane. He might be dead, Alice remembered, but for her. Her heart swelled up with pride and joy looking at the pair of them. It was almost too much to contain.

"Christmas!" she shouted. "I've never had Christmas before! Not like this!"

And Papa had promised her a wonderful present. She had asked, "How big is it? Is it beautiful? Is it useful? Will I like it?"

"Yes, I know you will. It's all those things. You will adore it!"

"And William too. Is it for him?"

"No, it's for you alone. And William has something very special which he will like very much."

"I've only got you something little because I've got no money," Alice said. She had bought him two cigars with money borrowed from William.

Papa didn't know about pocket money. There were things he still had to learn. But that didn't matter now.

Tom came out to take the horses, and when they went in they found William only just getting up.

"We've been up for hours!" Alice shouted.

But William only laughed and said how ghastly being out on the heath was when you could still be snug in bed. Mrs Carstairs had breakfast ready and Papa had a long thin parcel for William, which he gave him when they were finished.

"Alice has got to wait for hers, after church. It will be delivered."

Alice shivered with anticipation. She had never had a real big present before, only dear Goldie. She watched William tear his wrappings apart. From the shape he had already guessed, and his face brimmed with delight.

"It is! Oh Papa, the very loveliest thing! How marvellous! How wonderful!"

A fishing rod! And another parcel of boxes of odd fishing things, and a net and a pair of fishing boots. Alice was very disappointed, but saw that to William it was magical.

"Mr Scott always said it was a waste of time. I asked for a rod often, but he never gave me one."

"He never told me, otherwise you would have had one long ago. I love fishing too. Perhaps, tomorrow, we might call on my friend Harry over at Thurlow and try the rod out. He has a very well-stocked lake. And a stallion almost as good as ours, Alice, so if you come you won't be too bored."

Boxing Day. For Alice that had always meant a brisk walk in the morning and an afternoon spent reading the lives of the saints, the only consolation being that the saints did have very gruesome deaths: being grilled, flayed, torn apart by four horses or pitted with arrows. If the book had pictures, so much the better. But visiting stallions had never been on the agenda. Church, of course, even with Papa, was always on the agenda.

They walked to church. Tom would meet them afterwards with the trap. Papa said it was too cold for horses to wait outside for an hour and a half, and walking one way was good for them. *What a kind man*, Alice thought; Mr Ticino had had Daisy waiting hours for him in all weathers. No wonder Tom had the rheumatics. It was cold enough to be Russia. Was Mama already in St Petersburg, going to church in a fur hat to the sound of Russian bells? If she had been with them now, how everyone would have stared! Then Alice realized that today, going to church, was her first day out – publicly, officially – with her father and her brother. And if their mother had been with them, the whole congregation would surely have had the best Christmas present ever – scandal before their very eyes! Even without her, this day in church was going to be a great source of gossip over the Christmas lunch. Had William thought of it? She sneaked a glance at him walking on the other side of their father and saw that he was still aglow with the glory of the fishing rod. He looked wonderfully handsome and happy. Papa looked stern – he had thought of it, certainly, and was going to carry it off with magnificent unconcern. So, so would she. She belonged now, she had a place, and would hear no more hisses of "Alice Ticino". Not after today.

Their entry caused a frisson of excitement. Even the organist hit several wrong notes as the rustling and bobbing of turning heads distracted him, but Papa walked serenely to a place amongst the racing fraternity as if totally unaware. Alice kept her head up and, so that she might smile and not turn red, she thought of Robin on fat Daisy singing "Gwine to run all night!" She thought of her marvellous present still to come, and of Snatchcorn, and of having a mother. She arrived in her seat without any panic. Then Papa was close, and when they sat down he put his arm round her and gave her a quick hug, so she knew that he knew what she had been thinking. William wasn't bothered at all.

But the service was long and there was time to think, and Alice became aware that her father's thoughts were in Russia, and there was no way to comfort him. He did not sing the hymns, and when the prayers were for loved ones far away he shut his eyes and bent his head and a sort of quiver went through him. Alice could feel her tears rising, and swallowed hard. Having so much, she did not want to think of how much more she might have had. It was all too difficult. She had to think of her present again; it was the only way.

When they came out, Tom was waiting for them in the trap with Mother Goose. Mrs Pinney and Mabel came up and kissed Alice and bobbed to Lord Falkenburg, and Mr Ticino came up and pecked Alice on the cheek and shook hands with her father, and quite a lot of people smiled at them, and nobody now went past with their noses in the air. Alice felt wonderfully secure, belonging. Papa, having arrived, had given her new home stability. William had never missed this essential ingredient in his life and was now quite calm about the change in his situation.

On the way home he said to his father, "In church, I was thinking—"

"During the sermon?"

"Yes." William grinned. "I was thinking about school."

"Oh yes?"

"I think I will go back. There was a chap there who has a home on the River Test. He's really keen on fishing and asked me if I'd like to go down there some time. But I didn't like to say I hadn't a rod or anything. But now, well, I like him. It would be nice."

"Yes, you'll never meet chums if you stay at home with a tutor. You make friends for life at school and that's a great bonus. You'll be surprised, later on, how it gets you on in the world. And the first horrors — well, you're over the worst now. Another two terms and you will have quite forgotten."

"I suppose so," William lied. But he agreed that it would get better.

"You can always change your mind," Ralph said. "I had to do exactly as I was told and no one at home cared tuppence about my beatings and bullying, so I had no choice but to get on with it. That's why I would not order you to do what you don't want to. I remember the horror of it only too well."

"Yes, well, I've decided — I'd rather stick it out."

"Good lad. I'm proud of you. Church was not in vain."

William laughed.

When they got home, Alice rushed indoors to look for her present, but there was no sign of a big parcel in the hall, only a gorgeous smell of cooking drifting across from the kitchen. Mr Carstairs had lit candles on the mantelpiece over the fire and put some holly branches in a big vase. The red berries winked like fairy lights.

Papa said, "I can't see your present. Perhaps they've forgotten it."

"Oh no!"

"I'll ask Tom if there's been a delivery."

He went out again. Alice was mortified. Forgotten her present! But William was laughing. "He's only teasing you."

"What is it? Do you know?"

"It's something very nice. You will like it."

Alice had an inspiration. "It's a bicycle!"

She longed to have a bicycle.

"Perhaps it's a fishing rod!"

"My own trap for Mother Goose?" Some of the girls at school had their own traps. Alice rather fancied that. Papa had said it was big.

Papa came into the hall again, with much stamping of snowy boots. He was laughing.

"It's all right. It came while we were in church. It's out in the garden. It's rather big, so put your coat on again and come out."

Alice rushed for her coat and tore out of the door.

"Where? Where?"

She rushed round the corner of the house and there, standing on the lawn with Tom and Robin at her head, was a beautiful thoroughbred mare. She was a dark bay like Snatchcorn, almost black, with no white on her at all. She looked at Alice calmly, with large enquiring eyes. Alice was so surprised, stunned, that she stood stock-still with her mouth hanging open.

Papa came up quietly behind her.

"It's your own foundation mare, for your stud, Alice. Your very own. She will be Snatchcorn's very first wife – apart from old Daisy, of course. Her name is Dark Rosaleen, and she is extremely well-bred, and was a very sound winner a few years back. She is eight years old, in her prime. She will, with luck, breed you some beautiful foals."

"Papa!"

And she had thought it was a bicycle! She walked across to the mare and put her arms round her neck. Her coat was warm and soft with its dear, lovely smell, and she felt the soft muzzle nosing at her hand.

"She's a grand stamp of mare, Alice," said Tom. "You're a lucky girl!"

"Oh, she's gorgeous!" Alice breathed.

It was more wonderful by far than anything she could have imagined. For her own stud! So Papa was serious about it, not just joking her along. Dear Mother Goose for fun, Dark Rosaleen for serious business. And Snatchcorn . . . it was too much! She couldn't believe it.

"Oh Papa, you are so good!" And she turned and flung her arms round him. He held her close. She was crying with happiness.

"I'd rather have a fishing rod any day," William said.

They took the mare back to the stable. Dark Rosaleen had the box next to Daisy, and Mother Goose had been put down one.

"Until the new stables are built," said Papa. "The builders come in next week and we shall have a big yard behind this one, and a proper stallion box and a covering yard. We shall be so smart, Alice, and so busy. I don't how you're going to find time to go to school!"

What she would have to tell Henrietta! She gave Mother Goose a carrot to show she still loved her too, and then tore herself away because Mr Carstairs came out to say dinner was ready. Treat upon treat. Alice had never seen a Christmas dinner like it. Even when Mrs Pinney had done her best it had never been like this one, with every sort of vegetable and sauce steaming in silver dishes and the turkey itself nearly as big as an ostrich. For thin people, Papa and William were great eaters. If she ate like this often, Alice thought, she would be in corsets in no time. Mrs Pinney had threatened them long ago. Luckily Papa didn't know about that sort of thing. Robin in the kitchen would probably forget about being a jockey when this enormous carcass returned to their table.

What a day!

Later, after tea, when Papa and William were playing chess, she went out to the stables to say goodnight to her horses. To Snatchcorn, Daisy, Mother Goose and Dark Rosaleen. She could not say which one she loved the most. But her father buying her Dark Rosaleen meant that he was really serious about the stud. She loved the stables at night, the horses snug, rustling in the deep straw, the steady sound of munching hay signifying all was well. Outside, an owl called from the feed barn. It was still snowing softly, but scarcely lying, with stars fleeting here and there in the darkness.

I am lucky, thought Alice.

A year ago, she would not have believed this could happen

to her. And the future . . . one day her mother would come back to them. She knew it.

When she went in, it was late. William had gone to bed. Alice opened the door of the sitting room very quietly. Her father was sitting by the remains of the fire, staring into space. Alice had never seen a look of such sadness on a face before. It was grey with despair and longing.

She had no place in this scene. There was no comfort she could give. He did not want her. She closed the door silently and went up the stairs to bed.

She found it hard to get to sleep that night. Goldie stood on her bedside table, the moonlight winking on his metal coat, reminding her of his comfort when things were so bad for her. Perhaps she should give him to Papa as a sign that bad things got better and one day he would as happy as she was now. She knew in her bones that her mother would come. The ambassador would release her when he retired after St Petersburg. Even if it might seem an interminable time to her father, it would not truly be long. It might just be a couple of years.

For her the dream had come true, the arms embracing her and the cry of "My Alice!" ringing in her ears. She knew now who she was, not Alice Ticino after all, but Alice greatly loved in her own family.

She turned over, remembering Dark Rosaleen with a tremor of excitement, anticipating the thrill of telling Henrietta all about her wonderful present, and fell asleep with a smile on her face.

K. M. Peyton is the winner of the prestigious Carnegie Medal and the Guardian Award, and is the author of over fifty well-loved novels for young readers including the bestselling Flambards series.

Born in 1929, K. M. Peyton wrote her first book at the age of nine. It was called *Grey Star, the Story of a Racehorse*. Several books later, her first was published when she was fifteen. *Sabre, the Horse From the Sea* was followed by two more pony books written under her maiden name of Kathleen Herald. At first Kathleen only wrote pony books as, growing up in a London suburb, she could not have a horse of her own, so put her pony-obsessed daydreams down on paper.

K. M. Peyton lives in Essex with her husband Mike and her horses.

www.kmpeyton.co.uk

K. M. Peyton
Blind Beauty

"I have yet to meet a pony-lover who could resist K. M. Peyton's glorious books"

MEG ROSOFF

Every once in a while a great race horse is born
that will become famous throughout the land.
Buffoon is such a horse.

Tess senses something special in him, a hunger
for success as great as her own. And together,
they could go further than anyone would
ever have imagined...